"CROSSFIRE!"

Buchanan dropped to his knee. His right hand made the gesture of a master magician. His gun came out spitting fire and lead. He felt a burning across his left shoulder. He was slow in turning around.

Gunfire crackled: the smell of powder was acrid on the air. Arizona said again, "Crossfire!"

McGee was down. Buchanan had found him first, knowing his position, suspecting the plot. . . .

Fawcett Gold Medal Books
by Jonas Ward:

BUCHANAN SERIES

BUCHANAN'S BLACK SHEEP

Jonas Ward

FAWCETT GOLD MEDAL • NEW YORK

ONE

*F*ROM THE SLOPE OF THE BIG HORNS EASTWARD THE rain-wet plain below sparkled like a million jewels. It was a time of beauty, of contentment for Buchanan.

The hunt was nearly over. Coco Bean was trimmed down to fighting weight and ready at any time to defend his title as black prizefight champion of the world. Buchanan's big black horse Nightshade was lean and fit.

"Coco, you had enough?" Buchanan asked.

"Plenty," said Coco.

"How about you take the mule and the gear and ride down to that new little town. You know, named for the general. Sheridan."

"You goin' after that big moose?"

"I got to see him." His tracks in the morning dew had been unbelievably large. He was, Buchanan thought, the king of them all.

"You always say shoot to eat. Leave some for the coyotes and the birds. That's what you always say."

"Comes a time," Buchanan told him. "Comes a time."

"This here Montana or Wyoming?"

"Just barely Wyoming. Follow the trail, find us a place to sleep and eat. Sell the packhorse if you can. I'll be there soon enough."

"Shootin'. Always shootin'," grumbled Coco. "Ain't enough to fish."

"We ate fish and we ate venison. And it's time to quit," said Buchanan. "You want to go to town?"

"I'm more than ready."

So they parted. It had been the best of all possible vacations, the two old friends together. They enjoyed nothing more than each other's company. They had been through wars and entanglements and innumerable prizefight promotions and had not come out unscathed. They felt they had earned a break.

Buchanan rode through alder, beech and hawthorn. It was late summer and the landscape was lush. Small animals scurried. A lark sparrow trilled a long and varied song. Down below was a gully; he did not know its dimensions. Always the deep hoofprints of the moose led him on.

There was a ranch somewhere in this area below, in the fine grazing land where Texans had moved their big herds the better to fatten them for market. Cross Bar was its name, and its owner was Jake Robertson. It might be a good thing to visit Jake, a hard man but honest in his fashion, Buchanan thought. There was a daughter who had gone away to finishing school sometime in the past, a pretty girl. She would now be in her twenties. Time passed too swiftly on the western frontier. Buchanan sighed.

He had come up the trail at fifteen, a gangling kid, already the tallest of the range crew. He was orphaned, penniless. He fought, bit, scratched—and ate his way. Now he was six feet four and weighed 240 pounds, and people knew who he was. From Canada to Mexico the name Tom Buchanan was cursed or sworn by according to the lights of the individual in question.

He had encountered Coco in an El Paso jail where they were both falsely imprisoned and had broken out together. When that escapade was over they had become bosom companions. Coco had won all his battles in the squared circle. Buchanan had suffered wounds galore but had managed to survive his many fights on the side of justice. In the highest and best circles of the frontier West, the black man and the white man were pointed out as an unbeatable combination, a lesson for one and all to digest.

There had been a light rain in the mountains and now the sky was clouding over. The pace of the moose was slow and stately. Buchanan's eyes were on the ground, following the easy trail. His rifle was in its scabbard, and he had one revolver hiked high for comfort in his belt.

A black cloud scudded through the sky. There would be more rain. He picked up the pace. He was determined to catch the giant beast before the rain brought his hunt to an end.

There was a steep incline as he led Nightshade through the sage and odd, painted Wyoming cactus—the flower cactus—and through the wetness of it all. Buchanan dismounted. He was coming close now, all his instincts told him so.

At last the magnificent animal was in sight. Buchanan crouched, peering. A white-tailed jackrabbit scurried past him. He saw that the hunted animal was not a moose but a bull elk such as he had never seen. It must have weighed eight or nine hundred pounds. The head, neck and underparts were brown, the sides and back yellowish gray, shading to a tan patch on the rump and white between the legs. The antler spread was all of five feet. The elk stood majestically against the lowering clouds, nose pointed skyward. Rain fell. The elk did not stir. There were faint distant sounds, barely distinguishable above the soft patter of the rain. Buchanan arose. The elk ignored him, turning toward the disturbance, wrinkling its nostrils.

The sound of firearms pierced the thickening air. The rain increased, slowly, then with slanting force. The elk swung, altering his primary course, and trotted off as though disdainful of human violence.

Buchanan ran for Nightshade. He donned his slicker, pulled down the brim of his Stetson and rode cautiously toward the disturbance. He had no desire to mix in with a gunfight in strange territory, but curiosity always rode his shoulders.

Further, this was Crow country and those were Indians he knew and respected. He had friends among them. Texans as a rule did not understand northern Indians. They were accustomed to Comanches, Kiowas, Apaches, different breeds, usually hostile—sometimes with good reason and sometimes without reason. In his long experience he had learned a fundamental truth: Good and bad people came in all hues.

There was suddenly a downslope leading into a deep ravine. Nightshade delicately picked his way. Through the beat of the rain came a bleating outcry. Far above men shouted, gunfire echoed, a diminishing sound now, as if the task was completed.

Buchanan rode on, down, down. He was thoroughly aware of what had happened. At the bottom of the wooded ravine he came upon a flock of sheep—huddled, bleeding, shattered. There were perhaps a couple of hundred of them. It would be an abject lesson, he knew, a warning: No sheep allowed in cattle country.

There was a reason if not an excuse. He dismounted and did what he could, using his revolver to kill those who were suffering and could not recover. It was nasty, difficult work in the gloom of the evening downpour.

Cattlemen and sheepmen would always be at war. Grazing was the key problem. The sheep nibbled close to roots, damaging the crop for the current year and the next. Texas cattle were filling up the country now. Jake Robertson of Cross Bar was not a man to brook opposition.

Completing his unpleasant job, Buchanan stumbled over a small creature. It made a pitiful sound. He bent low and discovered it was a black lamb. He picked it up and examined it with care. There were no broken bones. It cuddled in his arms.

He bore it back to where Nightshade awaited and climbed into the saddle. The lamb was docile, frightened but probably starting to feel safe and sound.

There were sheep still alive in the ravine. They could be rescued. Buchanan had been a cattleman for much of his life, but here he felt injustice had been done, men destroying lives of animals without true cause. It was as if he had shot the bull elk and removed its antlers for a trophy, leaving the carcass for the coyotes and the vultures. He rode for town, cradling the little black sheep. The rain did not lessen nor did it improve Buchanan's temper.

Sheridan was a tiny new settlement. There was a wide main street, a stream over which a wooden bridge had been built, a few scattered houses, a general store, a hay-and-feed emporium and the inevitable saloon. There were a few lights, but the brightest came from the saloon. He tied up and walked in with the black lamb in his arms.

Coco was not present, probably putting up his horse and selling the packmule to the stableman behind the feed store. There were several customers, cowboys. Some of them were still damp from the elements. The bartender was a fat man with sideburns. They all stared hard at Buchanan.

He asked, "Would there be some milk in this joint?"

The bartender said, "You drink milk, mister?"

"For the lamb," said Buchanan. "You could warm it up a bit. It was cold and wet down in that hole."

"What hole?"

5

"Where these jaspers ran a herd of sheep," said Buchanan.

A lean, rugged man stepped forward. "Name's Dave Dare. Foreman for Jake Robertson's Cross Bar. Sheep ain't welcome."

Men formed a semicircle behind Dave Dare. The bartender looked the other way, remaining neutral, it seemed.

Buchanan put the lamb carefully on the bar. "Milk. Warm if possible. Name's Buchanan. Jake knows me."

"Buchanan, yeah. Heard of you. I still say sheep ain't welcome hereabouts." Dare was wearing a Colt. All the others were armed as well. Two of them ranged on either side of the foreman.

"Do tell." Buchanan surveyed them. They were Texans by the cut of their jib. "Only, you see, this ain't sheep. This here's a particular lamb half-grown. Right now it happens to be in my care. Poor little feller, he needs help."

"Hell, Buchanan, way I heard, you're a cattleman. What the hell you want with a damn sheep?"

"I make that none of your business," Buchanan said.

"Sheep's plenty of my business. Sheep is the ruination of my business."

"Heard that before. Howsome-ever, this sheep is my business."

"Then take your damn business elsewhere."

"Don't happen to be any elsewhere in this burg." He was hoping Coco would appear. He did not believe that this bunch would start a gunfight over one black sheep. Howsome-ever . . . He counted six of them. The odds were a bit too great against him. He played for time. "Wouldn't want any trouble. I've knowed Jake for a heap of time."

"Jake hates sheep worse'n loco weed. If you know him, you know that. Now take your damn critter and get it outa here," said Dare.

The street door opened and closed. Without looking Buchanan sensed that Coco had entered. He said, "Half-dozen of you, ain't there? Not enough. The sheep stays."

Surprisingly, Dare did draw his gun. He aimed it at the black lamb on the bar top. Buchanan moved like a bolt of lightning. One hand knocked the gun from Dare's grasp. The other clipped the foreman on the chin, knocking him back into the arms of his men. The two who had been closest charged.

Coco came on. Buchanan grasped the first pair by the nape of the neck, shook them, then banged their heads together. That left only three combatants.

Coco was beauty in action under such circumstances. He moved with the grace of a large cat. His fists were like iron. Ducking, swaying, he danced and pivoted. Not a hand was laid on him. He was the boxer-fighter par excellence.

Buchanan lounged back at the bar, one arm around the sheep, enjoying Coco's performance. The unfortunate cowboys went left, then right, then over a table, then against a wall. One made an effort to climb Coco's back. He was tossed off, then struck by a perfect left hook which draped him half over the bar.

Buchanan now drew his gun. As the hurt and confused cowmen staggered to their feet, he said, "This here is all nonsense. You got two choices now. You can belly up and drink on me . . . forgettin' about this here sheep. Or you can hightail it outa here and tell your story to Jake Robertson. You pays your money and you takes your pick."

Dare was rubbing his jaw. The others stared at Buchanan's gun and waited, wavering, looking to Dave Dare.

The foreman said, his voice a bit muffled, "Nobody's goin' into a shootout with you, Buchanan. And I ain't drinkin' with no sheepman."

"Not my sheep," Buchanan reminded him. "Just a little friend I made out there where you was doin' your dirty work. You tell Jake I know his problem but I ain't for

7

herdin' sheep over a cliff. You tell him I'll be out to see him.''

''I'll be damned if you're welcome.''

Buchanan said, ''Why, now, you bein' a Texan seems to me you'd know better'n that. You do like I say and you'll live to fight another day.''

They were all willing to go. Buchanan watched them file out, then said, ''Bartender. About that warm milk.''

''Sure, Mr. Buchanan. I was just waitin' till the dust cleared.'' The fat man bustled.

Coco asked, ''Now where did you get that purty li'l old lamb?''

''Down among the dead and wounded.'' Buchanan told him what had happened.

''You lookin' for moose and found sheep.''

''It was the biggest bull elk I ever saw. The sheep, that was just an accident.''

''Yeah. One of them accidents that gets us into all kinds of trouble.''

''You call that trouble, that little fracas? Seemed to me you were enjoyin' it.''

''Just a li'l workout.'' Coco was petting the sheep. ''He's a cute li'l devil at that, ain't he?''

The barkeep came with milk warmed hastily over a wood fire. Coco assumed the role of nursemaid.

''Name of Bascomb. I own the place,'' said the barman. ''That was a tough crowd you cleaned out, Mr. Buchanan.''

Buchanan pointed at Coco. ''Name is Coco Bean. You follow prizefights?''

''Certainly. Coco Bean. He's the champ. Made a few dollars bettin' on you, Coco.''

''This little critter sure cottons to your milk,'' said Coco. ''Could use a glass myself.''

Bascomb hastened to accommodate him. He said, ''That would be Shawn Casey's lamb. He's the only sheepman around. There was others, but they skedaddled when Jake Robertson put out the word."

"Casey, that would be the name of a man who didn't quit so easy," said Buchanan.

"Him and his daughter, they're purely feisty people," said the barman. "Got three thousand woolies. Got a half-breed named Peter Wolf with 'em and he *is* a wolf. You got yourself in the middle of a war, Mr. Buchanan."

"I knowed it," said Coco. "Every time we have a nice, easy time by our own selves it happens."

"I'm not lookin' for a war," said Buchanan. "Just couldn't leave this little fella out there among the survivors."

"Thing is, everybody around here is tetchy. The farmers, they don't hold with Cross Bar. Jake, he aims to be cock o' the roost come hell or high water."

The door slammed open. A tall, wiry, middle-aged man came in with a rifle at the ready. Flanking him were two companions with drawn Colts. One was a dark young man with aquiline, finely cut features and black, shining eyes. The other was a long-legged girl with braided dark hair, high cheekbones and flashing green eyes, a bold-looking girl wearing a man's checkered shirt and tight Levi's over riding boots.

The man said, "Stranger, that's my lamb. You drive my sheep over a cliff. That's bad enough. Now you steal."

Buchanan said, "Mister, if this poor critter is yours, by all means take him. Just figure I'm mindin' it for you."

Bascomb interposed. "Mr. Casey, this is Buchanan. And Coco Bean. They asked for milk for the lamb. And they just busted Robertson's crew all to hell, beggin' your pardon, Miss Casey."

The guns were lowered. "They beat up Dare and his crowd?"

"Mr. Dare and us, we had a difference of opinion," said Buchanan.

9

"There was six of 'em," Bascomb said. "It woulda done your heart good to see the fun."

Coco had not stopped feeding the lamb. "He's perkin' up real good. You folks want to sell the little fella?"

Shawn Casey leaned his rifle against the wall. The other two put up their revolvers—the girl wore a cartridge belt and holster, Buchanan noted.

"We owe you an apology," said Shawn Casey. "This is my daughter, Susan. My foreman, Peter Wolf."

"Pleasure," said Buchanan. "Drinks are on us."

"Accepted. Whiskey all around," said Casey. He had the diction of an educated man. "Sorry, these are perilous times in this country, gentlemen."

"So it would seem." He noted that Susan nursed her four ounces like a man. Her hand was shapely and strong-looking. Peter Wolf stood close by her, Buchanan noticed, and he did not blame the man. She was a shapely beauty, all right. Her eyes shone like precious stones. Her gaze was frank and direct—and curious. When she spoke her voice was throaty, deep, like that of a young man.

"You the Buchanan they tell about?" she asked.

"Reckon so, miss."

"You're a cattleman." It was an accusation.

"Not hardly. Rode the trails, sure. Owned a few head in my time. Nowadays I'm a . . ." He scratched his head and looked at Coco. "What am I?"

Coco said, "That depends. Sometimes you're my manager without no pay. Sometimes you're a huntin' man. Sometimes you're back there with Billy Button and our fam'ly. Most times, though, you buttin' into messes like this one."

"Lawman?" demanded the girl. She was more than a girl, Buchanan realized; she was a woman in her mid-twenties.

"Never wore a star but once," said Buchanan. "Didn't care for it."

"You're from down New Mexico way."

"You could say that. The high plain."

Casey said, "You seem to know a lot about Mr. Buchanan, girl."

"People sometimes talk to me when I get to the city. Buchanan, now, they tell tales about him."

"Can't stop 'em talkin'." Buchanan was not entirely at ease under her scrutiny. "Big talk don't mean anything."

"You're friendly with the Crows."

"That's true." She had probably heard of the big siege. That had been years ago, a very dangerous escapade from which a few Crows had extricated Buchanan and Coco. There had been an Indian girl with whom Coco had fallen in love. It was all part of the past.

The girl drank half her liquor. "The Crows have been friendly to us. It's the damn Texans who want to own the world."

"Not the world," said her father. "Just the graze."

"They've got no right," said Peter Wolf, speaking for the first time. "The land truly belongs to the Crow. The government took it from them."

"True," said Buchanan. "And the government leases it for grazing."

"Crow land."

"I don't say it's right."

Coco said, "Down south in the land of cotton it was *people* who was owned. Big war was fought about that."

The girl said, "It seems we are fighting our own war."

"Seems like the Indians and the sheep folk, they're like my people," Coco said, shrugging. "Purely outnumbered. Might makes right."

"Outnumbered," said Shawn Casey. "Yes, outmanned and in danger. But at this stage it's not merely the sheep. It's a matter of pride, of honor, of justice. We were here first. Robertson is the invader."

"He's a rotten bully and his daughter is a priss," said the girl. "His men are of the same mold as he."

"We are proud people," said Casey. "Truly they have the power. But just as truly we shall fight, damn their souls."

Peter Wolf said, "I only wish my people could help." He drew himself up and said directly to Buchanan. "My father was Crow."

"You must be proud." Buchanan inclined his head. "Now, about the baby, here. You want to take it home?"

Coco said, "I'd like to keep it for a pet." He beamed. "We could take it down to little Tommy Button."

"It's yours," said Shawn.

"And may we offer you beds for the night?" said the young woman quickly. "You are damp from the rain. We have hot water to spare."

"I do thank you," Buchanan said. "I was thinkin' of chowin' down at Jake Robertson's. Now . . . not a good idea."

He paid Bascomb for the drinks. The barman said, "Best if I keep quiet about you-all. Them Cross Bar men, they spout off too much around here. Scares a man tryin' to do business in a small town."

"Best you do as you say." The man would not be one to take along, but he could be a source of information. He seemed friendly to the Caseys, who struck Buchanan as being his kind of people.

There were three horses at the hitching rail. In the light from the saloon all seemed solid, well cared for. These were not ordinary sheep folk. They rode northward.

It was a ten-mile ride. The buildings were low against the flat land. There was a barn, pens, shearing sheds. The ranch house was of solid construction, low and sprawling.

A young Indian boy came to take the horses. The Caseys called him Johnnybear. Then a woman appeared in the doorway, tall and erect. She called, "Shawn, Susan, are you all one piece?"

"All fine and guests for dinner," said Casey.

The girl went ahead, vanishing as soon as they were indoors. The room was wide and deep and furnished comfortably in the fashion Buchanan had seen on eastern trips. There was a fire in a large fireplace. On the walls were paintings of the West. Buchanan recognized one or two done by Remington. It seemed an odd residence for sheepherders. But then, Bascomb had mentioned three thousand head, which was considerable if not huge.

Mrs. Casey acknowledged the introductions with a firm grasp. She had deep blue eyes and carried herself like a queen.

Casey said, "Buchanan and Coco had a run-in with the Cross Bar thugs. They brought the little black lamb safe to us. I gave it to them."

"It was really my lamb, but you're more than welcome," she said. Her smile carried truth. "I'm so happy the dear thing survived."

"It was a rotten sight," Buchanan told her. "Decent men don't do things like o' that. I'm plumb surprised at Jake Robertson. Never knew him to be that kind of hombre."

" 'Power tends to corrupt; absolute power corrupts absolutely,' " quoted Casey. "Lord Acton, 1887."

" 'Unlimited power is apt to corrupt the minds of those who possess it,' " said his wife. "William Pitt, 1766."

"My wife is of English descent," said Casey, smiling.

"Seems like I read that William Pitt supported the colonies durin' the Revolution," said Buchanan.

"Indeed!" Mrs. Casey showed surprise.

Buchanan said, "A man is alone a lot in the West. Some take to readin'."

Casey said, "Should we have a toddy and get acquainted? Susan . . . where are you, Susan?"

She came back into the room. She had changed to a flowing, flowered dress. Her feet were in matching slippers. The neckline was low enough to reveal that she was a woman properly endowed. She busied herself making drinks at a mahogany sideboard.

Peter Wolf went to help her. He seemed a welcome member of the family. His attitude toward the girl was plain to see. Whenever possible his hand touched hers, his rare smile was for her alone.

Casey was saying, "My ancestors were Scottish-Irish. When they migrated to America they went into commerce, but their background was in sheep. Wool for the mills, you know? It's in my blood. When we came west I found herders, imported good dogs, settled here. All was well until Robertson came."

"Sheep graze too close, leaves nothin' for cows. Been a problem ever since I can remember," Buchanan remarked.

"The farmers are friendly. After all, we were here before the Texans drove their cattle north." Susan was definite. "Robertson is purely a monster."

Buchanan said mildly, "Should be a compromise, some way of workin' it out."

"Not with that man and his bullies."

"Workin' cowboys, miss," said Buchanan. "They come tough or they don't last long."

"Robertson has brought in new men recently," said Casey. "I take it that means all out war. We are not ready for a war."

"I'm ready!" Susan was on her feet, gesturing. "If they can hire men, so can we."

Peter Wolf said, "I sent Gowdy out to bring in the livin' sheep in the ravine. He took Joe and they're carryin' guns."

"Who was guardin' the flock that went down?" asked Buchanan.

"Our dogs. They are the finest."

"I didn't see any dead dogs. Looks like Jake was just givin' a sign."

Susan cried, "They can't run us off!"

"I've considered moving on, maybe to Canada," said Casey slowly, quietly. "War is costly. No one ever wins."

"I say we hire fighting men," said Susan. "Mr. Buchanan? What about you?"

Buchanan shook his head. "My sympathy. But I ain't for hire. I can talk to Jake Robertson."

"What good will that do?"

"Know him. Know his kind right well. Fought for what they got, will fight more."

"Dirty, rotten, underhanded fighting," Susan said.

"Uh-huh," said Buchanan mildly. "It's plumb wrong. But he wouldn't see it thataway."

"What other way is there? Men with guns chasing sheep over cliffs!"

"Bad."

"And you sit on the fence?"

"Susan!" said her mother.

"The gal's right," Buchanan said. "A man has to take a stand. So—I'll see Robertson tomorrow."

"But you beat up his men," said Peter Wolf. "You'd best have company. I'll go along."

"Wouldn't work," Buchanan told him, smiling at him. "Thing is, Robertson's against sheepmen. He ain't against me."

"But his men . . . ."

"Texans don't back up gunners who go out of their way to pick a fuss," Buchanan said. "Coco and me, we're pretty well known for mindin' our own business."

"It won't do any good. They mean to run us out of the country," said Susan.

Her mother said gently, "I believe supper is ready. If you'll finish your drinks?"

A stout woman of indeterminate age served. Her name was Beth Bower, Casey said, introducing her. The food was plain, excellent and plentiful. Buchanan's appetite was more than healthy. He had been long away from food served from kitchen to table. Beth Bower regarded him, after his third helping, with respect and pleasure.

She said, " 'Bout time we had a man around who could appreciate my cooking."

Buchanan said, "Such food has got to be eaten." The woman was strongly built, plain-looking, with large violet eyes and blonde hair coiled about a shapely head. " 'Specially when it's prepared by such a handsome lady. And with such good company."

"I declare," said Susan. "Such fine talk."

Shawn Casey smiled, as did his wife. Peter Wolf was silent, frowning a bit as though pretty talk was not for him.

Coco murmured, "Oh-oh."

Dinner finally completed, they retired to the parlor. Buchanan noticed a piano in the corner of the large room. He said, "Music. Haven't heard any for a long time."

Without further ado Susan seated herself at the instrument. She ran a few deft chords with clever fingers, then played and sang in a pleasant, full voice, "Flow Gently, Sweet Afton." On the second chorus Buchanan joined in.

"A fine baritone!" said Susan. "Something lively?"

She switched to "Camptown Races," then to "Buffalo Gals." Beth Bower came from the kitchen and now everyone was joining in except Peter Wolf. He sat apart, expressionless, drinking wine.

It was a lively hour or two. Shared music made them feel warm and comfortable with one another. When it was ended, Mrs. Casey said, "Time for bed, I think. At least for Susan and me."

Buchanan nodded. "Been a long day. If we can use your bunkhouse?"

"Not at all," she said. "We have a room for guests."

Susan said, "I'll show you the way."

The room was an obvious addition to the original house. It was big and airy and contained two beds, a washstand, rawhide chairs, a Navajo rug, a closet. Susan looked around it with pride. "We love having guests. The farmers and their wives, an occasional traveler. It's a welcome change in our lives."

"It can get lonely out here. But you got a regular family," said Buchanan. "It's great country."

"It was before Robertson came." Her mood changed. "My father is not afraid, you know. It's just that . . . he doesn't want anyone hurt."

"I understand, miss," said Buchanan. "Let me talk to Robertson. Then we'll know more."

"We? You said 'we'?" Now she was smiling. "Oh, thank you, Mr. Buchanan. Thank you!" She fled.

Coco said, "Oh-oh!" this time audibly.

"Never mind your 'oh-oh's," said Buchanan. "These are nice people."

"Sure are. 'Specially the gal."

"Peter Wolf's sweet on her."

"I noticed."

"Just forget what's in your head," Buchanan told him. "I never did see sheep people like these. Usually they're out alone. They got their dogs. They move the flocks here and there for grazin'. They don't cotton to people much."

"They don't cotton to folks at all," said Coco. "They're mostly dirty. Nobody likes 'em. And they never do seem to have women."

"The Caseys are more like cattle people." Buchanan shook his head as he readied himself for bed. "Only different. This is goin' to take some thinkin' on."

"And you're goin' to do the thinkin'," said Coco. "Oh-oh."

"You got to try and help decent people. Besides, there's the black lamb. Gave it to us, didn't they?"

"Oh-oh," Coco said again. What he meant was that he knew from long experience that once again Buchanan was getting involved.

17

Buchanan thought about it as he drifted off to well-earned sleep. Someone had said that the reason the Lord loved sheep and sheepmen was that no one else could. The Caseys, he thought, were different. And who would not love the little black lamb he had rescued?

Then there was Jake Robertson, who had never given evidence that he was a bad man. Tomorrow would be another day, a day of discovering where Jake really stood, if it was his idea to run the flock over the cliff or if it was purely on the part of Dave Dare and his men.

He sighed. No question about it, he and Coco were into it, whatever it turned out to be.

TWO

COCO SNORED. BUCHANAN CREPT INTO HIS CLOTHING and carried his boots to the watering trough. He washed. The sky still threatened. He carried gun and revolver to the stable. He saddled Nightshade. He put the short gun into his saddlebag and holstered his rifle in the boot.

The Indian boy called Johnnybear appeared like a slim ghost in the light of dawn. Buchanan motioned him to silence, led him into a vacant stall. He spoke in the Crow language.

"I do not wish to be heard."

"I speak English," said the boy. He was slim and straight. His eyes were as black as his carefully kept hair. "You are Buchanan. My people know you."

"How old are you?"

"Fifteen. I am not a warrior. I have no name."

"Johnnybear'll do," Buchanan told him. "It's a good name. Have you been with the Caseys long?"

"When my people were killed, they took me. They are good to me."

"But you'd rather be back with the tribe."

"Sometimes yes. Sometimes no."

"Where is the closest encampment?"

"There." He pointed to the north and west. "Some are on reservation. Some not."

"Your own folks?"

The boy's teeth gleamed. "Dead. My cousin Walking Elk is not."

"I don't know Walking Elk."

"He is a brave."

"He makes war?"

"No. He hunts for the others."

Buchanan said, "Good. When the Caseys wake up, you tell them I am going to Cross Bar."

Johnnybear looked hard at him. "Without pistols?"

"Uh-huh."

"You are brave man."

"No. I'm a Texan."

"May the Great Spirit be with you." He went out of the stall and showed Buchanan a rough little box filled with straw. In it was the black lamb. It bleated weakly. "I will care for it. Maybe it is good luck?"

"Maybe," said Buchanan. He certainly didn't know—he knew next to nothing about sheep, black or white. "See you later."

He rode out. The close-cropped graze was dripping wet beneath Nightshade's hoofs and a mist rolled around in a fitful breeze. He kept on steadily toward the place where the sheep had gone over the cliff.

He heard the blatting, then smelled the wet wooliness, then a warning shot was fired. He reined in and called out, "Buchanan here."

A voice said, "It's him, damn it, Joe. Put up that gun."

Out of the white damp blanket of fog came two sheepmen

afoot. One was large and corpulent, the other thin and stooped. The latter still held a rifle at the ready.

The fat man said, "I'm Gowdy. This here's Indian Joe. He's plumb mad about what happened."

"Don't blame him," said Buchanan. "Only you're supposed to ask first, shoot second."

"I keep tellin' him. He ain't long for this world if he bucks up agin the Cross Bar. They got too many guns."

The Indian glared, silent, accusing the world.

Gowdy went on, "He's a Navajo. They're all sheepherders, ain't they?"

Buchanan asked, "How many did you save from the ravine?"

"Mebbe a hundred." Gowdy gestured. "Some limpin' but able. The little black lamb's gone."

"I've got him safe," said Buchanan.

"Good luck, I figured. Only one black this season. Well, it wasn't good for a couple of hundred. The dogs, they fetched us, then Peter, he sent word."

"Kinda dangerous out here for you-all right now."

"Yep. Reckon the other herders'll quit. Thinkin' about it my own self. Joe here, now, he'll stick."

The Indian grunted. His eyes were snakelike in the faint light of the early morning. He would be a fighting Navajo.

Gowdy went on, "Reckon if you're with us I could stick, too."

"Against Robertson's gunners?"

"We've got a couple tough herders, maybe. We got dogs."

"Dogs?"

"I got a couple dogs'll eat a man up in two minutes. Trained 'em since the Texans come. Me, I'm good with dogs."

Buchanan said, "There's a time and a place for every livin' critter, my pappy always said."

21

"I'm a sheepherder. But I ain't no pulin' yella-belly," said the fat man. "If Casey'll give us help, I'll stick."

"Uh-huh. You stick whilst I see Robertson."

"Talk is too late," said Gowdy. "They bled our sheep."

"Just so they don't bleed a man. I'll palaver with 'em," said Buchanan.

"Sure hope you come out alive." Gowdy was cheerful. "Man livin' with sheep, he ponders a lot. Joe, here he ain't half as good as the animals sometimes. You do what you think's best and let the Lord take care of the rest. Good luck, Buchanan."

Buchanan saluted and went on his way. Luck was one factor upon which he seldom depended. He thought he knew people, and in people he put his trust until forced to do otherwise. He rode to the place where the sheep had been driven over the edge of the ravine. The coyotes and the vultures were already at their work on the corpses. The stench was formidable.

He searched for tracks. There had been six men in Bascomb's bar. He counted six horses in the raid. Dare had admitted the deed but Buchanan wanted to make certain with his own eyes. He knew enough about Robertson to make sure of every detail before facing the Texan.

He counted the resistance fighters with Casey. There was Peter Wolf, the two herders and . . . the girl, Susan. She had worn a gun and put her whiskey down straight in Bascomb's. It remained to be seen how many hard men worked for Robertson and how they might be expected to act.

Past the ravine the grass grew taller, as if Casey had kept his sheep from that section of the prairie. Either that, thought Buchanan, or riders from the Cross Bar had guarded the acreage. There was a goodly stretch of it but not enough for an ambitious cattleman with a large herd. Robertson would not be content; he would be bringing more and more beef to be fattened in the coming season.

A truant sun arose and the mist began an upward spiral.

There were trees dripping from the dampness and the bowl of blue sky native to that country began to take shape. In the near distance Buchanan could see the outlines of Jake Robertson's Wyoming fortress.

It was indeed that, made of rough-hewn native stone and heavy timber. It was a big house. When Texans built something they planned it to stand forever, Buchanan thought not without some pride. Although he called New Mexico his home, he had been born in the Lone Star State.

There was a herd of longhorns, fat, eating their heads off. There was one man riding, lazing in the saddle. There did not seem to be guards against anticipated attack, and for good reason, Buchanan thought. As he grew nearer he saw a large bunkhouse, a corral, a barn, all the trappings of a successful cattle operation. It was early enough for Cross Bar to be at breakfast, a fact he had counted upon. He rode to a hitching rail in front of the impressive establishment and tied up.

He walked toward the house and called. "Jake Robertson. Buchanan here."

Men came hastily from the rear, the kitchen, Dare was in the lead; others he'd met the previous night were swallowing food as fast as possible. All bore bruises. There was a seventh man, bigger than the others, Buchanan's size. His sleeves were cut off at the shoulders, signifying that he was the smithy. He wore a black curly beard and a fierce expression.

Dare yelled, "That's him, Cobber. That's the one. He had a black man just as bad with him."

The smithy came to the fore. His arms dangled, corded with muscle. He said, "You goin' to use that rifle or fight like a man?"

"Why should I fight you? Never saw you before." Buchanan stood with feet apart, grinning.

"You ain't met one like me," the smithy told him. "You beat my pals. See if you can beat me."

"Aw, now, I wouldn't want to do that." He saw the man tensing for the rush. He started to turn away.

The big man lunged. Buchanan stepped aside. Down went the blacksmith over Buchanan's boot.

Dare shouted, "He's tricky, Cobber."

Cobber got up. He came on more cautiously, arms raised in imitation of a professional fighter. Buchanan shook his head in amusement. He had boxed hundreds of rounds with Coco. He let the smithy come close, then feinted with his left and dug a right to the body, stepping aside, then back in. Ducking under a wild, weak swing, he slapped Cobber once, twice, three times with his open hand. The big man's beard wagged back and forth.

Buchanan said, "Don't go outa your class, man."

Cobber roared. He rushed with wide-open arms, intending to grab Buchanan in a bear hug. Buchanan allowed him to do so. Dare and the others howled with glee.

Buchanan flexed his shoulders and arms. Cobber's grip slipped. Buchanan elbowed him away, pushed with his palm. The smithy fell full-length from the force of Buchanan's shove.

Dare hollered, "Okay, boys. Get him."

The six were about to make a concerted rush. Buchanan skipped to Nightshade and pulled the rifle from its scabbard. He said, "One at a time. Maybe two. That'll cut it."

Dare was choking with rage. Cobber got up and started another bull rush.

From the veranda of the big house Jake Robertson called, "That's enough fun for one mornin'. Git back to your breakfast, you darn fools. Come in and light and have somethin', Buchanan."

Dare said, "He's got it comin' to him, boss."

"He's got a lot comin' to him," said Robertson. "Seems to me, though, you boys ain't the ones to do it, without guns."

Dare shuffled his feet for a moment. Fury was in him, but

his discipline was strong. He led the men back to the rear of the house. Cobber stared hard at Buchanan for a long moment, then went along with the others.

Buchanan went to the veranda. Robertson was a medium man, brown-haired, florid from good living, sporting a bit of a belly beneath his belt. He exuded good humor, health and wealth. Yet Buchanan knew him for a tough, scheming businessman. In many ways he was typical of the cattle baron. He had started with a wide loop among the long-horns, stole or bartered for land, fought nature, Indians, hoof-and-mouth disease and bad weather.

Jake Robertson had come home from the Civil War to find his father slain and his mother and sister barely able to make ends meet. He had won a horse and saddle in a poker game and the rest was history. When it became good business to move north, he had come to Wyoming, where every spring the cattle had been driven from the southland to fatten on the better graze.

He had built a fine house, two stories high, a wide veranda all about, everything a native Texan would want in a strange country.

"Betcha ain't had breakfast," Robertson said.

"Can't say I have," said Buchanan. "How are you, Jake?"

They shook hands. "Pretty good for an old man."

"Old you ain't. Mean as a snake you are," said Buchanan.

"Right as rain. Have a mornin's mornin'?"

"Don't mind if I do. It was chilly out there lookin' over the dirty work done by your men."

Robertson motioned to a rocking chair. "Aw, come now, Buchanan. The boys seen it all. One of them dumb damn sheep starts over a cliff and the rest follow lickety split and away they go. You know that." He filled two glasses on a tray containing liquor and a pitcher of water. "That fella Casey, he's too refined-like for the West."

25

Buchanan sipped. "Fine whiskey. Y' know, Jake, a man gets to know how to read track after a while. I mean the way horses act when they're runnin' and when they're just moseyin' along with the rider observin' what's happenin'."

"Simple as A-B-C." Robertson smiled.

"Your boys were chivvyin' the sheep."

"Aw, now!"

"Besides which, I heard the shootin'."

Robertson drank. "You heard something. Then you went into Bascomb's with a damn black lamb and beat up on my boys. You and that nigger champeen of yours."

"We don't call Coco a nigger. And he ain't my anything except my very close friend," said Buchanan, staring into Robertson's eyes.

"Oh. See what you mean. A special nig . . . er, black fella."

"A friend."

"Okay. Okay. I apologize all to hell." He chuckled. "When the boys told me they'd run agin Buchanan and I seen the damage, I had to think back."

"I'm a peaceable man," said Buchanan. "Everybody knows that."

"You are, you are. Never knew you to start a rangdoodle. Never knew of one you couldn't finish."

"I got the scars to prove it." Buchanan finished his whiskey. His stomach was rumbling. A bell rang indoors.

Robertson said, "Time to set."

There was a large parlor furnished from the best stores. Beyond it was a dining room long and bright. The oaken table was covered with fine linen. The odor of biscuits and bacon was in the air. A tall woman with severe features and a tight hairdo stood in the kitchen doorway with arms folded over her apron. Light footsteps rapped on the stairway descending to the hall. Buchanan paused as a young woman of twenty-odd entered, smiling, hands outstretched.

Robertson said, "You remember my daughter, Claire?"

Buchanan took the two tiny hands. "Lordy me, I remember a slip of a gal, shy as a bunny rabbit. Looky you now, lady!"

She was diminutive. She was blonde and her skin was fair and delicate, rosy and white velvet. Her eyes were as blue as Wyoming skies. She wore a dainty informal gown with a high neck and long sleeves. She was beautiful. To Buchanan, she looked like a Dresden doll he had seen once in a Frisco museum.

She said, "You haven't changed. It's so good to see you again. Please sit down and have your breakfast."

"Yeah," said Robertson. "Show Miz Bacon here that you can chow down with the best."

Buchanan bowed at the housekeeper, who responded by lifting one dark, thick eyebrow. Then she vanished to reappear with a silver tray loaded with eggs and hot cakes and syrup and sizzling bacon. Buchanan seated himself and began the serious business of filling his aching void.

Robertson said, "You note Claire's manners and all? Sent her to the best schools. She took to it like a duck to water." He beamed fondly upon his daughter.

"Now, Papa." She had dimples, too, Buchanan saw. She addressed him, still smiling. "I was watching from upstairs when Cobber attacked you. You were wonderful."

Her father said, "You shouldn't look at sich things. By gum it cost me a herd of the finest beef to make a lady outa you. I just got to get you away from here to where there's company fit for you."

Over a forkful of food, Buchanan saw her jaw tighten, saw little lines appear on either side of her shapley mouth. To himself he said, All is not gold that glitters, eh?

"I have no wish to be elsewhere," said Claire.

"You can't go out in the sun without a bonnet," Robertson said. "You're just too delicate for this country."

"I am not delicate." Her chin hardened. "Please, Papa, let us not discuss it any longer."

27

Robertson swallowed hard. "Yes, my darling. We ain't in agreement, but you're my pet, always and always."

Her mouth relaxed, the smile, complete with dimples, reappeared. A calculating expression crept over the countenance of her father. He spoke to Buchanan.

"Old friend, how'd you like to roost here for a spell? Bring your black friend along. We got a spare room ready for any good ol' boy, and he can sleep in the bunkhouse."

Buchanan said, "Mighty nice of you. No, thanks."

"There's plenty huntin' and fishin'."

Buchanan said, "Truth to tell, I'm stayin' with the Caseys."

"You what? With sheep people?"

"Sheep people and niggers," said Buchanan, riled. "That's what it is, and I like it a heap."

Claire said sweetly, "I think Mr. Buchanan is absolutely right. He knows who his friends are. Really, Papa!"

Robertson muttered, "It ain't natural. A cowman."

"Just think on it," said Buchanan. "Coco among those men of yours? Why, he might damage them real bad."

Robertson did not reply. Conversation died at the table. Buchanan ate enough to make Mrs. Bacon relax and give him a tiny smile of approval.

They repaired to the veranda. Robertson resumed with the whiskey, Buchanan politely declining. Claire had a dainty piece of material on which she was working with shiny needles. Her hands were strong and capable.

Robertson said, "I got a couple thousand head up here. It takes some doin'."

"You're keepin' them close." Beyond the outbuildings Buchanan could see a herd in green fields.

"Not all. I got men you ain't seen ridin' 'em."

"Leased land?"

Robertson was evasive. "I lease from the gov'ment."

"Casey has a lease, also."

"Oh, sure."

"Seems like the lines get erased sometimes."

"Ain't it always thataway?"

Buchanan asked, "Would you be willin' to sit down with Casey and talk things over?"

"Confab with a sheepman? You loco, Buchanan?"

"He seems a right nice gent," Buchanan said. "Talks pretty, like Miss Claire."

She said, "Thank you. Miss Casey, I understand, actually carries a gun."

"Miss Casey needs a gun when some men are around."

"Like that breed that lives with 'em? Haw," said Robertson.

Claire's busy hands on the tatting stopped and her jaw again thrust forward. She said, "Papa, that is no way to talk."

Buchanan said, "Peter Wolf? Seems like a nice enough fella."

"I'm sure he is," said Claire. Her voice was clipped and cold.

Robertson tossed off his drink, poured another. He said, "You ain't insinuatin' agin *my* boys now, are you?"

"It's a rough country." Buchanan strove to pass it off.

"Sheep are so smelly." Claire smiled, but her hands were slow in regaining stride. "Stupid, too, aren't they?"

"Like some people, they follow the leader," Buchanan said. "Never was much for 'em myself."

"But you're takin' up for the Caseys." Robertson's tone was testy, combative. "Don't seem right to me, Buchanan. Maybe you got your eye on the gal."

"Papa!"

Buchanan unfolded his length from the chair. "Well, I do thank you-all for the fine grub. I better be gettin' along."

Robertson snarled, "I ain't settin' down with no sheep people, man, woman, nor child. Tell that to your friends."

"Sorry about that," said Buchanan.

"They want a war, they'll get a war."

"They positively don't want trouble of any kind," Buchanan told him.

"Then let 'em take their goddam sheep elsewhere."

"Papa!"

Buchanan said, "Good day, folks." He walked down to where Nightshade patiently waited. Claire got up and tripped along beside him.

Her father yelled, "Good riddance to ye, sheep lover."

"It's the liquor," the girl said. "Please forgive him."

"No harm." Buchanan looked down at her. Now her cheeks were flushed and her determination was plain to be seen.

She said, "Peter Wolf. I've met him."

"Uh-huh." A dim light went on inside his head.

"Is there . . . are he and Miss Casey . . . involved?"

"My dear, I only met them yesterday."

"I found him very . . . interesting."

"Uh-huh. Handsome fella."

"Nice." She paused, then said, "I'd like to know Miss Casey. After all, we're about the same age. I mean she's a couple of years older, maybe, but . . . Papa would never consent."

"Your papa purely hates sheep and those who run 'em."

"What Papa doesn't know wouldn't hurt him." Her chin was firm. "Supposing I were to visit you, an old friend? Tomorrow?"

"Well, I ain't quite sure I'll be there. . . . Get this straight, though—if I stay, it'll be to help the Caseys out of a tight spot," Buchanan said.

"I hope you do!"

"You sure?"

"I'm against killing sheep. I'm against fighting neighbors. I want us all to live in peace," Claire told him.

"Uh-huh. In that case it's up to you. No reason you can't visit me at Casey's place."

"Thank you. I thought you were that kind of man. I remember the tales about you from when I was a child."

Buchanan winced. The girl had been born a mere dozen years after him. "Well, thanks."

"I'll see you tomorrow, then."

He touched his hat brim and rode back toward the Casey place. Obviously there was more than Susan Casey's friendship occupying the pretty head of Claire Robertson. It took little imagination, plus his observation, to conjure up the image of Peter Wolf. It took no divination at all to know what would happen when Jake Robertson was confronted with the situation. There would be fire in the mountains.

Perhaps he should have discouraged the girl on two counts. There was what he had observed about Peter Wolf in regard to Susan Casey. He could not be certain on such short notice, but indications were that the half-breed's attitude was more than brotherly love.

On the other hand he had not noted a warm response on the part of the girl. On the third hand, he reminded himself, it was none of his doggone business. In matters of romance he believed in freedom of choice, devil take the hindmost and several other philosophies better not thought on too hard.

If the girls did hit it off, maybe some good would come of it. Jake was a hidebound bigmouth but never had seemed an evil man. Shawn Casey was more than willing to have peace.

He put these thoughts in the back of his mind and rode across the plain with the notion of surveying the overall scene, of locating the flocks of sheep and their keepers. He always wanted to know the exact details of the terrain in which he was operating.

In the distance he could make out another herd of cattle. He unlimbered his old field glasses, won from a cavalry captain in a poker game long ago. These were crossbreeds with Hereford blood, finest of beef cattle. Horsemen guarded them, riding slowly, slouched in the saddle. He could see Dave Dare lounging beneath a tree.

He rode north. After several miles he found the sheep, a sea of wool, a cacophony of blatting, mewling noise. A single shepherd watched over them, but several dogs walked alertly about and among them. They were short-haired dogs, black and white, with sharp noses and alert ears.

A rider detached himself from the scene and rode toward Buchanan. In a moment he recognized Peter Wolf. They met and reined in.

"Buchanan," Wolf greeted him.

"Peter Wolf." This was to be a formal meeting, Buchanan sensed immediately.

"Are you staying?"

"That depends."

"On what?"

"On a lot of things. Like, can I get Casey and Robertson together? So far I've failed."

"Robertson will not palaver."

"You knew that."

"Any fool would know it. He wants all." Wolf swung an angry arm. "The graze. The country, all of it."

"People like Jake do get too big for their britches," acknowledged Buchanan. "Still, he ain't all bad."

"Bad enough. If you stay, will you fight him?"

"My aim's to get through all this without a fight."

"Will he pay for the sheep his men killed?"

"That I doubt."

"You see?"

"They claim they didn't stampede the sheep."

"And you? What do you think?"

"They lie."

"Then he pays."

"Maybe he believes 'em."

"Robertson? He told them to do it."

"You don't know that."

32

"I know it. I know it in my guts."

"So you'd hire gunners and go after Cross Bar."

"I'd hire them to make sure there's no more killin'."

"Might stop the killin' of sheep. But then you'd have people killed."

"Damn the people. They get in the way, they take their chances. That's the way it's been, hasn't it?"

"Uh-huh," said Buchanan. "No reason why it has to keep on bein' that way."

"Go talk to the Crow," said Peter Wolf. "See what they think about it."

"Why don't you talk to them?"

A dark cloud settled on the face of the young man. "I'm a breed. White people—outside the Caseys—don't want anything to do with me. Indians don't accept me either."

"You had schoolin'."

"A little schoolin's a dangerous thing."

"Uh-huh. You learn just enough to know we can't know everything we want to know. Didn't have much schoolin' my own self. Up the trail at fifteen. Like I said last night, though, I read a lot."

"It ain't enough to read. This country has been stolen from the Crow and their cousins by the government. Now it's bein' stolen again by a devil from Texas."

Buchanan said, "Bein' ain't windin' up." He was looking at a stand of willows bordering a stream coming down from the hills. There was motion, then there were riders. He swung up the glasses even as he called, "Watch out," to Peter Wolf.

The riders were bareback. They wore breeches but no shirts. Even at his range Buchanan could see they were youths, young braves. Nightshade went into top speed from a standing start. Peter Wolf followed.

The dogs immediately began circling the herd of sheep. The herder picked up a rifle and fired. His aim was bad.

Over his shoulder Buchanan yelled, "Don't shoot."

Peter Wolf, riding a small bay, was far behind the swift course of Nightshade. Buchanan rode a circle, heading for the trees. Two Indian boys swooped down on a sheep, picked him up between them and uttered a shrill war whoop as they turned for the copse of woods. The others lay back to head off pursuit, brandishing bows, quivers of arrows slung over their shoulders.

Nightshade made the Indian ponies seem as if they were standing still. Buchanan cut between the sheep thieves and their destination.

He sat there, looming, imposing. He did not draw revolver or rifle. The pair with the sheep, intent upon their difficult task, almost ran him down. When they discovered him, they came to a jolting, sliding stop.

Buchanan said in the Crow language, "You will return the sheep to the herd."

For a moment it seemed they would try to fight. Their brethren, a half-dozen of them, came within arrow range, saw Peter Wolf advancing with rifle in hand and paused. It was a standoff.

Then the two youths dropped the sheep, which blatted in disgust and trotted to where a dog was eagerly seeking to chivvy it back to the herd.

Buchanan said, "Since when do the Crow steal sheep?"

The leader of the outriders came closer. "And who are you who speak our tongue?"

"I am Buchanan. Go tell your chief. Tell him I will visit him and smoke the pipe."

The young Indian said, "I am Walking Elk. I do not know Buchanan. We are hungry. The man from Washington does not feed us well."

"Then ask for what you need," Buchanan told him, his voice harsh and strong.

"From the white man? Ha!"

"Do you know the white man who owns the sheep?"

"We know the white man who owns the cattle."

34

"Then you know only half. Now, go and do as I say."

They milled about. They stared at Peter Wolf, curled their lips. They jabbered among themselves, careful, however, since Buchanan understood their language, to reveal nothing.

The leader said, "Buchanan. I will remember."

"See that you do."

Reluctantly, with many a glance cast backward, they rode off through the woods. Buchanan found himself grinning. He looked at Peter Wolf and for the first time caught him with a rueful smile.

"Boys will be boys," said Buchanan. "Since they ain't at war, they got to do somethin' to prove themselves."

"Stealin' is all they know."

"Tell the truth. Would you have given them a sheep to eat if they had asked?"

"No," said Peter Wolf. "But Shawn Casey would."

"There you have a lesson," said Buchanan. "Think it over."

He rode off toward the Casey ranch.

THREE

PETER WOLF WATCHED BUCHANAN CANTER AWAY ON
the black horse. He had not come off on top in the meeting
with the Crows under young Walking Elk, Johnnybear's
cousin. He wrestled with his pride. There was much on his
mind these days.

There was the problem with Susan; this was at the top of
his mind. The Caseys had never referred to his mixed blood,
had accepted him as an equal, yes, as a member of the family. It was all in his head, he had told himself repeatedly.

Yet he knew what other people thought. He knew the
scorn of both whites and Indians. It was seldom patent, on
the surface, but it was always present.

Then there was the matter of his debt to the Caseys. They
had been wonderful to him. He owed them a lot. If Jake Robertson or any of his cohorts were to harm a Casey, he
would make them pay. If there were to be a war, he would
be in the van.

Added to this was the disturbing matter of Robertson's

daughter, that seemingly frail, small blonde lady who could ride like the doughtiest cowhand, who was devious in her ways, who appeared when least expected, who asked embarrassing questions, and who stared him down when he avoided giving answers.

He mounted the bay and rode toward the herd guarded by Gowdy and Indian Joe. Twisting in the saddle, he could see Buchanan riding for a high place, as if to observe the countryside. It did seem as though the big man was concerned about the Caseys. Peter Wolf's loyalty had to be with him.

On the other hand were the exchanges between Susan and Buchanan. Or at least there had been interest on Susan's part. Peter Wolf's sensitivities in that direction were excruciating. He swallowed hard and went on.

Indian Joe and Gowdy were on the job. The dogs were enjoying their work, keeping the herd in order.

"No sign of trouble," said Gowdy.

Indian Joe grunted. "Trouble soon."

"Buchanan?" asked Gowdy. "Is he with us?"

Without hesitation Peter Wolf said, "Yes."

"You sure?"

Peter Wolf lied. "I talked with him. He is with us." That would hold them in line, he thought. "Get word to the others at the north herds."

"Oh, we'll do that." Gowdy beamed. "With Buchanan on our side anything can happen. He's one *hiyu* man."

"Yes," said Peter Wolf.

"He's fought more fights than any man you ever heard of. He's sweet-talked more women than you could shake a stick at. He's the friend everyone needs, by gum."

Indian Joe said, "He even good to Indians. Sometimes."

"He's good to good Indians," Gowdy said.

"Yes," said Peter Wolf, wincing inside. "We've heard about Buchanan. Plenty."

"That friend of his, he's a champeen."

Peter Wolf said, "Two men won't cut it. I hope Buchanan will bring in some fighters." Since they were so high, it might be well to give them more hope.

"Them Crows, now. What about 'em?"

Peter Wolf made an instant decision. "I will go to them."

"That's a good idee," said Gowdy.

Going ahead, following his instinct, Peter Wolf said, "I'll take them a sheep. You got a troublemaker?"

"Got a mean one, all right. Old Mabelle, we call her. The dogs don't like her. Troublemaker."

"Point her out."

She was a middle-sized animal with one wall-eye. They walked around the herd. The dogs chivvied her until she was apart from the others. Then Peter Wolf drew his knife and slit her throat.

"You takin' her home?"

"No. I'm takin' her to the Crow."

"Do tell!" Gowdy was respectful. "That takes nerve."

"It may work to our good," said Peter Wolf. He strung the carcass over the pommel of his saddle and rode westward. He knew vaguely what he was going to do. He followed trail. It was a long way to the clearing among the trees. He could see the hilltop against the skyline when he rode in. He imagined the figure of Buchanan, the omnipotent, watching from on high.

When Peter Wolf reached the clearing, Walking Elk came to face him. They were of equal size; indeed, they somewhat resembled one another, the high cheekbones, the finely chiseled features, the rather full lips, the dark, brooding eyes deepset, the black brows fierce across the brow. Peter Wolf threw down the dead sheep. On a spit above a banked fire, a quarter of beef sizzled—Cross Bar beef, no doubt.

He said, "I see you do not need my offering."

"We always need," said Walking Elk.

There were more of them than Peter Wolf had expected to see. They sat on their haunches, bows and arrows, and a few old guns near to their hands. They stared at him without blinking.

He said, "There were dead sheep in the arroyo for the taking."

"Yes?"

"But you tried to steal one of ours."

"Not yours, Peter Wolf. Theirs."

"Shawn Casey is a good man."

"No white man is good. Why else are we forced to steal?" Walking Elk spoke in his native tongue.

Peter Wolf answered in kind. "You are not forced to steal from Shawn Casey."

"We steal from them. We will do whatever we can to hurt them. We will do so until they learn we are not to be despised." Walking Elk's voice rose, the black eyes burned. "You are half-Crow. You cannot tell us what we must do."

"I am not telling. I am saying that the Caseys are good. They have taken care of Johnnybear, your kin. They have given me a home. It is Robertson the cattleman who is threatening to take all of the land. He is the enemy."

"True, he is an enemy." Walking Elk agreed. "So is the great Buchanan. So are they all."

"But you fear Buchanan." He should not have said that, he knew, but made no effort to retract it.

"And you, a half-breed? You do not fear him? You fear them all. You come running to us to talk for the sheepman. The sheepman is afraid of the cattleman. Buchanan? He alone is not afraid."

"Your chief is a friend to Buchanan."

"Our chief is old and weary. All our elders have fought and been beaten by the whites who took our land. We respect them. But we have our lives. We are not afraid as you are, half-Crow."

Peter Wolf dismounted with careful ease. "I am Crow enough for you."

"Ha!" They all laughed with Walking Elk.

"I never lived on a reservation. I am alone. Try me, O brave of the Crow." He hung his gun belt on the pommel of his saddle. He removed his knife from its sheath.

Without warning Walking Elk sprang at him. Peter Wolf stepped easily aside and put out a foot. Down went the Indian. Wolf circled, waiting. The brave bounced like a rubber ball and was again on the attack.

Peter Wolf met him. They locked together like fighting moose. For a time they wrestled on even terms, twisting, writhing. Walking Elk swung his torso and Peter Wolf went flying against the trunk of a tree. Dazed, he staggered forward.

Walking Elk closed in. Shaking off the fog, Peter Wolf met him with a straight right fist thrown from the shoulder. Walking Elk went wallowing backward.

Peter Wolf drew a breath and waited. Now the Crow circled him, his eyes afire. They went around and around, each seeking an opening.

The watching braves were silent except for involuntary yips as one man or the other dominated. None made an attempt to interfere.

They sprang together, locked each other in deep embrace. It was strength against pure strength now, each striving to crush the wind from the other. They staggered, went to earth. Peter Wolf clamped his legs around those of the Indian. He twisted an arm free, secured a wrist. He pivoted and was on top. He rolled over, using a trick he had learned from white boys. He brought Walking Elk's arm back in a hammerlock, maintaining the leg hold. Now he called on the muscles he had developed at hard work.

Walking Elk was helpless. Teeth shut tight, sweat pouring from him, he did not utter a sound. He was a brave; he would die before admitting defeat. Peter Wolf applied just enough pressure. Bone creaked but did not break.

Peter Wolf released his hold, came to his feet in one graceful motion. Walking Elk tried to arise, could not. One arm dangled. He staggered forward. Peter Wolf pushed him gently away and said, "Enough."

"Never!"

"It is not to the death," Peter Wolf admonished him. "We put aside our weapons. It is simply that you now respect me. If I am half-white . . . I am also half-Crow. You will remember."

There was silence. Walking Elk breathed hard, but the rules were strict; his men were watching. His lips thinned to a tight line as Peter Wolf buckled on his gun belt, picked up his sharp blade and mounted the bay pony, then spoke to them before he left. "I tell you that Shawn Casey and his family are good people. They would never harm anyone who does not first attack them. I tell you that the cowman is out to grab everything. That is my message. If you need sheep to eat, ask and it will be given to you. That is all."

He rode away. Walking Elk called after him, "There are no white eyes worth saving. They must go!"

On the hilltop Buchanan had been able to witness most of the encounter. He put away his field glasses and watched as Peter Wolf rode back toward the Casey house. He saw another horse cutting the angle to intercept the breed. He quickly brought up the field glasses, preparing to ride down in case he was needed.

He focused on the stranger. His eyebrows popped. It was Claire Robertson, riding hard, attired in jeans and boots, totally unlike the crinolined creature of the Robertson ranch house. There was no doubt that she was determined to speak to Peter Wolf.

"Now here's a pretty kettle of fish," Buchanan said to no one unless it was Nightshade. "The boy's in love with Susan Casey. And the Robertson girl's in love with the boy, or thereabouts."

* * *

41

Peter Wolf touched his hat brim and said, "Miss Claire."

"How nice to run across you this way, Peter." She drawled a bit so that his name came out like a caress—"Pe-eeterr."

"That's a fine filly you're ridin'." It was a well-bred black, contrasting with her blonde aura. He was always a bit uncomfortable speaking with her.

"Papa picked her out for me in Texas." She patted the neck of the animal, not taking her eyes from Peter Wolf. "You haven't been by to visit."

"Me? Visit your place?"

"Why not?"

"Why, Miss Claire, your people ran our sheep into a ravine. You sure must know that."

"Papa says they stampeded. You sure that isn't the way it was?"

"Yes'm. I'm sure." She could not be that innocent, he thought, but she knew how to draw the cloak around her, wide-eyed, staring at him.

"I hate it," she said, her chin creeping forward. "I purely detest this goin' on between neighbors. There's plenty of room for everybody in these wide-open spaces."

"True. Seems like your pa don't think so."

"My papa is a decent honest man. I'm going to do my best to bring your people and him together," she declared.

"What about those gunmen at Cross Bar?" Peter Wolf asked.

Claire tossed her blonde curls. "They mean nothing to me. Papa thinks he needs them. I do not."

"Buchanan's been to see your pa."

"Buchanan fought with our smithy. Buchanan may be a hero to some, but I think he's a big bully."

"He's been right polite to Shawn Casey."

"He's got no right meddling," she said. "Come, ride a ways with me. There's a pretty little creek yonder. I'd like to wade a bit. I purely love wading barefoot in a clear creek.''

''You mean that pretty little stream that runs down the lower pasture?''

''Yes, that's the one.''

He gathered up his reins. ''Miss Claire, that creek was polluted rotten by the sheep that were run over the cliff by your men. Good aft'noon, Miss Claire.''

He wheeled away and rode for the north camp, where another thousand sheep were grazing under the care of a few herders and many dogs. She sat staring after him, with tears in her eyes. Her chin was no longer hard. Her lips trembled. She sat for a moment in deep thought, then her head came up and she rode back toward the home ranch.

As for Peter Wolf, he rode around the entire perimeter of the land occupied by the Casey sheep. He talked to the men, heartening them, insisting that Buchanan was there to protect them all. Most had heard of Buchanan; those who had not were regaled with overblown tales of his heroics.

Peter Wolf accomplished what he wanted; he got the message out so that it traveled throughout the countryside. It would get to Bascomb's in Sheridan and thence to the outlying farms, to the Indian reservation, eventually to Cross Bar and Jake Robertson. That was the way of it in the places where there were no daily newspapers. News went with surprising speed by word of mouth.

That he was not telling the whole truth did not disturb Peter Wolf. The Caseys needed Buchanan. There was nothing in the world Peter would not do for the Caseys—and particularly Susan. Night after night he lay awake dreaming of her. He could never express his feelings to her, of course. He could only long for her with every ounce of his mixed blood.

He had spent time in a mission school. He knew that his destiny was his own to make; they had impressed that upon him. He also knew the prejudices of the West of his time, knew them too well.

He came to the Casey stable at night. As he stabled his horse, Johnnybear appeared. The boy had the true Indian faculty of moving like a silent creature of the wilds.

"I will take care," the boy said in the Crow language.

"It is good."

"Did you go far?"

"As far as I could."

"You spoke of Buchanan?"

"I did." He could not lie to the boy. "I made promises."

"He is here."

"Yes. I saw the black horse."

"Did you speak with the brothers?"

"Your brothers. Not mine." Bitterness was in Peter Wolf's voice.

"They will not help?" Johnnybear asked.

"They will not."

"The farm people?"

"They are afraid," Peter Wolf said.

"Buchanan might make the difference?"

"Might. Not surely."

"Aieee," said Johnnybear. "I fear for our patrons."

"Well you may." Peter Wolf touched the boy's shoulder and went into the house through the back door. He went to his room. He could hear music. Susan was again at the piano. She and Buchanan were singing songs he did not know and laughing together. They were able to put aside the thought of danger. He washed himself and changed his clothing, then went to the kitchen.

Mrs. Bower heard him and came with a warmed-over dinner. "You're late, young man. I saved pie for you."

"I was busy." He sat down. The music rang in his ears. Susan was playing for Buchanan; he sensed it.

44

Shawn Casey came into the kitchen. "You rode far today."

"I talked with people."

"The Crow?"

He shook his head. "Not good. The farmers are scared. Without Buchanan we will be beat."

Casey said, "I never believed the others would help. They have their own troubles."

"I had to try."

"Of course you did. Come have a drink and relax, Peter."

"Mrs. Bower has pie for me." He managed a grin.

"When you're ready." Casey smiled at him, nodded and returned to the parlor.

Mrs. Bower said, "It'll be a sad day when Robertson's gunners come."

"You women should leave," he replied darkly.

"Susan, she'll never leave, come hell or high water. And it won't happen overnight."

"If we don't get help, it'll happen quick, all right."

"The good Lord will dispose," she told him. "The Caseys are good people."

"You ever see good people die?"

"I've seen aplenty in my time," she said. "I plan to go on a good while yet."

"Oh yes, I hope for that, too," he said. The pie was delicious, but his stomach was delicate tonight. He toyed with the crust, took his time about finishing.

After a time he went quietly into the room where they had gathered. Coco had a fine, velvety voice. He was singing a song about the South. The others were chorusing as Susan picked out the melody. Buchanan boomed, doing his best, though he was no singer. Susan was smiling up at him. Peter Wolf poured himself a drink of red wine and retreated to a corner, brooding.

* * *

In the Cross Bar bunkhouse Dave Dare and Cobber were sharing a bottle of hard cider. Cobber bore few outward signs of his fight with Buchanan, but inside the scars were deep.

"Never did see a man could stand up to me," he growled.

"They say the black's even better than Buchanan. I swear they're both alike as peas in a pod," said Dave Dare.

"Gimme another chance at him and I'll kick him to death."

"You may get a chance at that. If'n he sticks around with the sheepmen, he's bound to get in range."

"You'd shoot him." Cobber flexed his big hands. "I just wanta get a hold on him and crunch him."

"Might meet him in Bascomb's come a night. You never do go to town with us'ns."

"I'm up before dawn fixin' your damn horses and wagons. I ain't for drinkin' too much no ways. I would go in if I knowed he was there though."

"Mebbe we can arrange it." Dave Dare's mind worked it over. "Set a watch. Find out when he's goin' into town."

"Might do." Cobber clenched a fist. "You've killed men, Dave. With your gun."

"When they needed it."

"I could kill him with my hands."

"Guns are cleaner."

"When they die. . ." Cobber stopped, started again. "How is it when you hate a man and you see him die?"

Dave Dare thought a moment. "Y' see, it's him or you. I mean with the gun. Him or you. So you shoot. If you're quick enough . . . But I'm no gunfighter. Ask Boots or McGee. It's their game."

"I never killed a man. Oh, I've beat 'em to a pulp. Never knew one to die."

"That's the difference. With bullets they die. Gene'lly

46

speakin', that is.'' He drank heartily of the hard cider. ''Best we go in and eat. The others'll be done by now.''

''I ain't hungry.''

''You will be. Come, now.''

Cobber arose. ''Aye. You're right. Must feed the inner man. Tomorrow's another day and all.''

''We'll get Buchanan one way or t'other.''

Jake Robertson's voice came from the doorway. ''Not your way.''

They stared at him. He was slightly drunk but in command of his faculties. He went on, ''You'll not bushwhack Buchanan. 'Tain't my way. You'll not run the goddam sheep when he's within a mile or more. You hear me?''

''He . . . he beat us. With his fists.''

''He's whupped better'n you. I ain't for him the way he is now, with the goddam sheep people. Howsome-ever, I know him. I know who he is and what he is. The less truck with him the better. You understand?''

''We got rights. Private-like,'' said Dave Dare. ''A man comes in, does what he done . . . We got rights.''

''You're workin' for me. You want to draw your pay and go for Buchanan?''

''Well . . . no.''

''You like your jobs?''

''Course we do. You're a good boss.''

''Then you take orders. Could be Buchanan will leave. Could be he don't want no part of a sheepman war. He's always been cattle, all his life.''

''He don't show no sign of leavin'.''

''He just got here. Give him time. If he makes trouble enough, then we'll see to him.'' He hiccuped and added, ''And God help them that get in the way. If we have to get Buchanan, I'll see to it. I'll plan it. Not you, not anybody in Wyoming. Me.''

Dave Dare said, "Okay, boss. If that's the way it's got to be."

"That's the way." Robertson turned and lurched away.

When he was out of earshot, Cobber said, "I be damned if I'll miss a chance."

"I'm with you," said Dave Dare. "He's the boss, but a man's a man."

"In town. Mebbe we could make it that Buchanan started it."

"There's Boots and McGee. We'll confab with them."

They were a different breed from Dave Dare and Cobber. It was in their walk, their carriage, the way they looked. Boots Semple was small and wiry, curly-haired and swarthy. Hap McGee was middle-sized and wide-shouldered. They wore dark shirts and tight black pants. Their guns were tied low on their flanks, their boots were soft and well kept.

It was their eyes that caught one's attention, though. Unblinking, they seemed lidless, like the eyes of snakes. The eyes of McGee were dark and deep. Those of Semple were light and wide-spaced. They said little, even in the bunkhouse among the other cowboys. Neither was much with a rope; they were very careful of their hands. But they could ride and they could—and would—shoot.

Dave Dare said, "The boss said to stay away from Buchanan."

"Yep," said McGee.

"We figure we owe him somethin'."

"Yep," said McGee.

"You listenin' to the boss?"

"Yep."

There was a silence. Then Cobber asked again, "How is it when you kill a man?"

"He's dead," said McGee.

"Is that all there is to it?"

"Yep."

"It don't seem . . . bad?"

"Nope."

Dave Dare said, "Come on, Cobber. We got to eat."

They departed. The other riders working nearby the ranch disposed themselves about the spacious, well-kept bunkhouse. McGee and Boots Semple strolled out under the starry sky and leaned on the rails of the corral.

Semple said, "They're plumb scared."

"Yep."

"You mind the time Buchanan gunned down Billy Watts?"

"Yep."

"Billy had his gun half outa the leather."

"Yep."

"You ain't scared."

"Now, that's another horse, pardner."

"Careful?"

"Yep."

"Takes two?"

"Yep."

"He's that fast. So we work together. We stay close. One at his back."

"Which one?"

"Whichever."

They were silent, staring at the horses quiet in the corral. The moon threw a fitful light upon them. A night bird trilled a song.

Semple said, "Mebbe Buchanan'll ride on. He moves around a heap."

"Mebbe he won't," said McGee.

"We downed a few fast ones in our day."

"Yep."

"Funny, that big ox askin' how it feels."

"Lotsa muscle. No brains," said McGee.

Semple gestured toward the bunkhouse. "They don't know. How it starts and all. Fella comes atcha. You got to down him. Then another. Then another. You're quick or you're dead."

"Yep."

"After a time it don't bother you none. You keep your eye peeled. You keep your gun loose."

"Yep."

Semple laughed deep in his throat. "You hope there ain't too many Buchanans around."

McGee said, "You'll be ready for Buchanan. He ain't all in all. He's been hit."

"With a rifle. And from behind."

"Yep," said McGee. "Either way's okay by me."

Semple proffered his makings and they rolled cigarettes. They were silent, each with his thoughts on Buchanan.

The clearing in the forest was lighted by a fire and the moon. Shadows flickered across the serious faces of the young Crow braves. Walking Elk sat apart, arms clasped about knees. He had been disgraced in the eyes of the men he led. He was waiting for the inevitable challenge.

The others did not speak. There was only one who could face Walking Elk. His name was Crazy Bird and he was taller and stronger than the others. He was blood brother to Walking Elk. The tension mounted as the moon made its orderly way across the sky. Still there was silence. The odor of cooked meat was strong. Birds called to one another. Small creatures nosed curiously on the edge of the camp.

Walking Elk arose and walked to the fire. His left arm was swollen; there were bruises on his face and body. Still he stood tall, facing the others.

He said, "The half-Crow's medicine was stronger than mine. What would you have me do?"

Crazy Bird stood. "Walking Elk behaved with honor."

There was a chorus of assenting grunts.

"Walking Elk led us when we took the guns from the white farmers. He has kept the spirit of the fighting Crow alive. I have no wish to fight him."

Again there was assent from the youths.

"We do not wish to return to the reservation. The old ones, as Walking Elk has said, sit in their tepees and mourn the past. We are the future. So long as we may stand we will fight the white eyes."

Now there were yips of assent. Walking Elk's eyes shone. He held his right hand high. "My brothers, if you want, I shall still lead you. We shall do our part to drive the whites from our land."

They all leaped to their feet and surrounded him, patting his back, being careful to avoid his injuries. Again they were of one mind.

They sat around the fire then and talked, making plans, discarding them, eating bits of the fragrant, sizzling meat. Walking Elk nursed his aches and pains and silently, secretly dreamed of again meeting Peter Wolf.

FOUR

THE MORNING WAS BRIGHT AND FAIR. BREAKFAST WAS cooking in the Casey kitchen. In the stable Johnnybear worked with currycomb and brush on Nightshade, cooing to the big black horse in the liquid syllables of the Crow tongue. Coco was feeding the little black sheep from a bottle. Buchanan was oiling his revolvers.

Peter Wolf came to them and said, "You know about my meeting with Walking Elk."

"Uh-huh," said Buchanan. "Too bad."

"I did what I had to do. They'll never give up. They should be sent back to the reservation."

"No way that I know," said Buchanan. "They look at it like we're all wrong. It was their land."

"Was ain't is," Coco said. "Had a preacher man tell me one time that my people were mighty big in Africa. Seems like that don't matter a bit now, does it?"

Peter Wolf said, "So we have to fight Indians and cow people just to keep on livin'. It don't seem right."

52

Buchanan put up his weapons. He went to where Coco was feeding the black lamb. He watched for a moment, his face softening. "Seems like it's a losin' battle, don't it?"

Coco said, "This is the purtiest critter ever. I purely love this little lamb."

"Best we should eat," said Buchanan.

"If you could send for help . . . ?" pleaded Peter Wolf.

"Jake would send for more'n I could raise," said Buchanan. "Can't you see that?"

Coco agreed. "Next thing you'd have two armies shootin' up the countryside."

They left the stable, going to the house. Johnnybear, eyes wide, had listened with care. He worked more slowly over Nightshade. There were tears in his eyes.

At the table Shawn Casey awaited them. Mrs. Bower, smiling at Buchanan, dealt out hotcakes, bacon, eggs galore. Only Peter Wolf failed to do justice to the heaping platters.

Shawn Casey said, "It's a grand day. Maybe we should ride out and see what we can see."

Buchanan said, "I think we'd better stay close this mornin'."

"Any particular reason?"

"Seems like we might have a visitor."

"Really? Anyone we know?"

"Nope."

"A mystery guest?"

"Not so much mystery. Still and all, some good might come of it. Just maybe."

Coco said to himself, "Oh-oh."

They finished the meal and went outdoors. The sun was hot, but a small breeze made the day lovely. Coco went to play with the little black sheep. Johnnybear went into the kitchen. Peter Wolf was restless, walking back and forth.

He said finally, "You didn't get Robertson to say he'd come to talk, did you?"

"Not a chance," said Buchanan.

Casey said, "Since there is nothing terribly important for us to do at this moment, shall we retreat to the veranda?"

"Good notion," said Buchanan.

They sat and stretched their legs. Mrs. Casey and Susan came, wondering, to join them. Susan wore her jeans, as usual, and a boy's shirt. Peter Wolf cast a glance at her, frowning a little to see the two top buttons undone.

Mrs. Casey asked, "A holiday, I hope?"

"Sorta," said Buchanan.

"I'd like to hear about some of your adventures," said Shawn Casey. "There have been rumors and tall tales. The truth."

"Nothin' much to tell," said Buchanan. "Coco, now, he's had some wondrous bouts with strange fighters."

"Me and Tom, we've seen a few elephants." Coco chuckled. "All the way from Canada to Mexico we been into it."

They talked easily, self-deprecating, dwelling on the humor of their experiences. Time passed, the sun ascended almost to its noonday peak. A rider appeared on the horizon. Peter Wolf jumped, eased his revolver around on his hip.

"Won't be needed," Buchanan assured him.

In a moment Susan said, "I'll be bought for a goat. It's herself, Miss Priss."

Claire Robertson came up on her fine filly. She wore a long serge skirt and a bright red basque jacket. Her hair was caught back in braids. She was riding sidesaddle today, one knee hooked over the curved, padded bar of a horn. One tiny boot was in a stirrup. Buchanan came down from the veranda and held out his arms. She laughed and jumped, displaying a shapely ankle.

"Thank you, sir," she said.

Shawn Casey came to his feet. "Welcome, Miss Robertson. It's good to see you."

Mrs. Casey came to hold out a hand. Coco was on his

feet, grinning. Peter Wolf stood, but there was no joy in him.

Casey said, "Have you met Peter Wolf?"

"I believe we have seen each other when riding," said the girl.

"Uh . . . yeah," said Peter Wolf.

Buchanan suppressed a grin. They seated themselves and Mrs. Casey called for tea. Susan sat on the top step of the veranda and stared hard.

Claire said, "It's long past the time I should have made my manners. The unfortunate incident of your sheep and the ravine and all . . . I'm truly sorry."

"Nice of you to say so," said Shawn Casey.

Claire regarded Susan, returning her curious gaze. "We should see each other often, you know. There are only two of us in this vast region."

Susan drawled, "True, true. Just we two."

"I'd like to have you over for supper," said Claire. "All of you."

Buchanan smiled. "Best ask your daddy about that. We had some words, remember?"

Claire bridled. "I am the hostess at Cross Bar. My papa will be polite to my guests, any guests."

"You reckon?" Buchanan nudged Coco.

The black champion said, "Seems your papa told Tom here that he don't cotton to niggers."

She smiled at them. "Uncle Tom Buchanan had a few words to say about that. Papa respects his opinion."

"I'm sure you mean well," said Mrs. Casey quickly. "But we have been attacked. A social meeting might prove embarrassing to all."

"I'm afraid I must agree with my wife," Shawn Casey added. "I would like very much to meet with your father. There is always a middle way, a compromise that may be reached. I would welcome a conference."

Claire's chin hardened. "I want you to know I am against

55

violence. I believe in good neighbors living in harmony. There is plenty of room in this country for everyone."

Susan snapped, "Tell that to your papa."

"I have told him and I will do so again."

"Tell him to get rid of his killers."

"He does not hire killers!"

Susan whooped. "Please, Miss Robertson. Boots Semple? Hap McGee? To say nothing of the others who follow the leaders like . . . sheep!"

"They are cowboys."

"They are gunmen," said Susan coldly. "Cowards who kill sheep."

Buchanan said mildly, "This ain't gettin' anyplace. There's a solution, you all must know."

"Barbed wire," said Susan harshly. "Line out the boundaries and run a fence. Stay on your side."

Now Claire looked shocked. "Barbed wire? Why, that's one of the reasons Papa came here from Texas. Barbed wire!"

"You've got an open mind about everything that doesn't interfere with your Texas ways, haven't you?" said Susan. "You come up here with your cattle and right away Wyoming becomes Texas and you own it."

Buchanan interposed again. "Now, ladies, no good to get personal. Lots of people are set in their ways. Mr. Casey, he's got the right notion. A meetin' with your papa might do some good. Jake Robertson ain't a bad man. I'll guarantee Mr. Casey. Tell that to your papa, Claire."

"I'll be glad to," she said. "I came here to be sociable. To make friends. I see I've failed." The chin pointed at Susan. "I know you are good people. This squabble should be stopped before it goes any further." She flashed her eyes at Peter Wolf. "If you will be so kind as to see me to my horse?"

Peter started, managed to control his confusion. Susan laughed. Buchanan arose but Peter walked past him. Claire took his arm and dimpled, looking up at him. She bowed to the others and swept down the veranda steps.

"La, la, la," said Susan, her voice not subdued. "Looks as if Peter has made a conquest."

"Shhh," pleaded her mother.

"Good for both of them," Susan went on. "The cowgirl and the sheepman."

Peter gave a hand to Claire's shapely boot as she mounted. She smiled down at him and he stood motionless, expressionless. She spoke a few words indistinguishable to those on the porch. She waved a hand and was gone, riding gracefully despite the awkwardness of the posture demanded by the sidesaddle.

Mrs. Casey said sharply, "Really, Susan."

"You're being unkind," added her father.

"She's a priss," said Susan. Peter was walking toward the stable, his head erect, his shoulders stiff. "Look at him. She's got him upset, now."

Casey said, "A priss she is not. She is an intelligent young lady. I believe she meant well."

"Well, ain't any question about that," said Buchanan. "Truth is, her papa inhales a lot of booze these days. Claire's got responsibilities. But you got to remember, in Texas the head of the house is master of every little bitty thing goes on."

"McGee and Semple are gunmen. You know it; I know it," said Susan. "They ran our sheep into the ravine. Now she comes mealymouthin' and tryin' her fancy ways on us. You believe in her. I don't." She stormed into the house.

Buchanan sat with the elder Caseys. For a few moments they did not speak. Buchanan's mind was going around. He saw complications he did not wish to face; he saw danger, a storm gathering, black and ominous, on the horizon. He had seen Claire and Peter together and knew that the young man had been cool to the girl. He had also observed that without question Peter was enamored of Susan Casey. He knew the

57

breed from which Claire had come, the die-hard tough Texas breed. He was well aware of the pride of Peter Wolf.

Mrs. Casey said, "I believe the girl wants peace."

"Yes," said her husband. "But Susan mentioned the bad word."

"Bobwire," said Buchanan. "Poison to Texas cowmen. They claim it keeps down expansion. Open range made them big. Bobwire and nesters cut into their style."

"There are farmers hereabouts," said Casey. "Homesteaders, really, but I suppose Robertson would call them nesters."

"Peter said they wouldn't help us," Mrs. Casey reminded him. She looked at Buchanan. "Have you decided to stay?"

Buchanan lifted a shoulder. "Can't say for certain. I tried to talk to Robertson. I can try the farmers. What about the sheriff?"

"Never on hand," said Casey. "Always on county business. Name of Bromberg. Sheridan's too small to have a marshal. I believe there's a constable."

"It's a hard proposition for you people," Buchanan admitted. "If I could help . . . Don't exactly know how. You people have been mighty good to us. Coco and me, we'll take a ride about."

Coco said, "There's the little black sheep. I purely love the critter."

"A symbol?" Casey smiled. "A little lamb shall lead us?"

"It don't hold together." Buchanan smiled. "Black sheep, that ain't a lamb to lead. Howsome-ever . . ."

"And I should ride the north herd," said Casey.

They went to the stable. Susan's voice, high-pitched, reached them.

"You do your work and I'll do mine, Peter Wolf. Or would you rather be meeting Miss Claire? Please do. She's sure got her cap set for you. Maybe you can talk some sense into the heads of the Robertsons.''

Buchanan coughed, then he and Casey made a clatter and walked in. Peter Wolf, stony-faced, was riding out. Susan flung after him, ''If you're one of our family, which you should be, you'd know how we feel about you. That's enough!''

He rode off, still silent. She whirled around and glared. ''Eavesdroppin', were you? I purely don't care. I've got no interest in Peter Wolf . . . that way.'' She flushed. ''It's not that he's half-Indian. It's—just the way things are. All of you better understand that.''

Her father said in his gentle fashion, ''Of course we understand, Susan. I'm just sorry you're embarrassed.''

''I'm not embarrassed!'' She tightened the girth on her frisky young chestnut mount. ''I'm mad clear through. First that priss, then Peter tellin' me he don't care a fig for her. A fig? Where'd he get that talk? I purely want to be left alone . . . and for us all to be left alone to do what we're supposed to do—raise sheep!''

She mounted and was gone in a cloud of mud clods as the horse pranced through the wet ground. They stared after her. She rode like a westerner, loose in the saddle, her long hair flying out behind her.

Coco said, ''She's a fine gal, all right. Trouble is, she got a short fuse.''

''And a strong mind,'' said Casey. ''Too strong, sometimes. You know, Buchanan, I should pull out of here. We could drive the sheep to more friendly grazes. We'd lose some; there'd be hardship. No one would buy this place, knowing Robertson. But at least we'd have peace and quiet.''

Buchanan shook his head. ''In the West we're plumb short on peace and quiet. Seems like if 'taint one thing it's another. You got a mighty fine place. You built it. Comes trouble a man's got to stick and hold on tight.''

''It's the women I'm worried about.''

"Naturally."

"They don't deserve this trouble."

"Few people do."

"If there was the slightest chance . . ."

Buchanan sighed. "We'll ride. When we come back, maybe we'll have news."

"I can't truly ask you to stay. The odds are too great."

"If Tom makes up his mind, there ain't no need to ask," said Coco. "That little black sheep, he brought Tom in." He scowled and added, "If it only could be done without no damn guns, now."

Buchanan was buckling on his cartridge belt. He slung his rifle into the scabbard, then said, "Without guns in this country at this time a man's naked and in trouble. Casey, keep your eyes open and your weapons ready. We'll be around for a day or so, at any rate."

They rode out. Casey looked after them, a man unsure of how to proceed, unafraid for himself but fearful for his family. He started for his saddle, stopped. He went slowly back to the house, where his wife and Mrs. Bower would be alone if he departed.

Johnnybear, busy with his chores, was glum. He fed the hogs and went to the henhouse, holding his nose. He began the disagreeable task of cleaning, careful to put aside an egg or two. Even the hens were careless sometimes, he thought.

The Caseys were like children in some ways. Buchanan was the hope of the Casey sheep ranch; Johnnybear knew that much for sure. He was all Crow; his instincts were pure. He was only a boy, but he could think things through. He only doubted what course he might take, if any. He knew he could never repay the Caseys for their kindness toward him.

Buchanan, he thought, it all depended on Buchanan.

Coco said, "Where we headed?"

"The herd," said Buchanan. "Just checkin'."

They rode toward the graze attended by Gowdy and Indian Joe. The sun was still high; the sky was bright blue. Clouds tumbled in a high wind.

Coco said, "That Miss Claire, she got eyes on Peter."

"You don't miss a thing, do you?"

"Miss Susan, she got eyes on you."

"Now, Coco . . ."

"And Peter, he got eyes and everything on Miss Susan. Oh, me."

"I swear, Coco, you been readin' too many of them little blue books that come with Bull Durham. And you don't even smoke."

"People leave 'em around. Now that you helped with my readin' I take pleasure in 'em." Coco laughed. "This here's like one of them plays by Mr. Shak-a-spear."

"That's Shakespeare."

"Smart fella. Writes funny sometimes. But smart."

"He's been dead a long time, Coco."

"Do tell! Didn't I see there was a play by him last time we was in Frisco?"

"Uh-huh. They still do his plays."

"Now, ain't that somethin'." Coco was wistful. "You think folks'll remember some of the shows we put on? In the ring?"

"Why not? People have writ about 'em."

"Sho 'nuff." Coco was pleased.

They came to the sheep camp. Gowdy greeted them. He was carrying an old Sharps rifle.

Buchanan said, "I see you're ready for trouble."

"Since we learnt you all were stayin' we been heartened," Gowdy said. "Indian Joe, he's over the other side of the herd there with a Remington and a long knife. Tell me, you goin' to bring help?"

Buchanan dissembled. "Can't say. You hear anything at night?"

"Not as yet."

61

He unlimbered his field glasses. Far south he thought he saw a group of riders. He motioned to Coco to follow and set Nightshade in the direction of the horsemen.

Before they could come close enough for him to recognize anyone, the riders turned and rode swiftly back toward Cross Bar.

"What you think that means?" asked Coco.

"I dunno. Maybe Jake's got notions. Maybe he wants us to go away before he tries anything again."

"Ho," said Coco. "Looks to me like we can't just up and leave, huh?"

Buchanan said seriously, "Looks like we got ourselves into somethin' we might not get out of."

"What about them farmers Mr. Casey talked about?"

Buchanan rode back to Gowdy. "Are there farms within twenty miles or so?"

"Sure. Nesters, whatever. Doin' good. They'll be next, though, if they only knew it. Yonder there's a few." He waved an arm. "They won't do nothin' to help. You can bet on it."

"We can try 'em."

"They prob'ly never heard of you, Buchanan. It makes a difference, knowin' who you are."

It was probably true, Buchanan thought, sighing. A man got a name, it went around and about, up and down. There had been a few gunslingers who had heard of him and had tried to kill him for the sake of their own reputation. He had reluctantly dispatched them. On the other hand, he was known to most people as a peaceable man. He never wore his gun in town unless there was definite danger well known to him and to others. He truly sought nothing but peace and quiet. The trouble was that the land was new, the law seldom effective until too late and the people fiercely independent because they were thrown on their own.

The first farm, twenty miles northward, was owned by a man named Eph Browning. He was plowing when they rode to the edge of his field and waited. He wrapped the lines around the plow handles, wiped his sweat away with a red bandanna and came to them, introducing himself, a pleasant man in bib overalls, soiled boots and a straw hat with turned-down brim.

When Buchanan gave his name, the man smiled and said, "Oh, yeah. Heard about you from Bascomb. You two walloped them riders from Cross Bar. Them fellas insulted my wife and daughter one time. Bad men."

Buchanan said, "They're threatening the Casey sheep. Stampeded a herd, did you hear?"

"We heard from Peter Wolf. Mr. Buchanan, we know about sheepmen and cattle people. Always a-warrin'. We aim to mind our own business, stay out of it."

"I was thinkin' of a meetin'," said Buchanan. "Call everybody into Sheridan, talk things over. I note you've got no fences. Maybe bobwire would sorta settle things down. Bring some kinda order."

Browning shook his head. "Way I hear it bobwire causes more fightin' than sheep agin cattle. You won't find a single farmer agrees with you."

"Would you spread the news, anyway? I might could get Jake Robertson to a meetin'."

"All right. I'll send my boy Andy around. Believe me, we want peace. We don't want cattle runnin' over our crops. But us people, we stick to ourselves. Mainly Yankees, we are. From New Yawk, my own self. Just tryin' to raise crops to feed a family."

"If the sheepman loses, you'll be next," Buchanan promised him. "I'm from Texas; I know the breed. They don't mean to be bad in their hearts, but they do breed a heap of cows. They need room, or think they do. An acre to a cow, and they got thousands of cows."

" 'Sufficient unto the day the evil thereof,' "quoted the farmer. "I do thank ye for comin' by. Got to get 'er plowed by nightfall.'' He lifted a horny hand and returned to his team.

Coco said, "Can't blame the man. He's no gunfighter."

"I ain't lookin' for guns. I'm lookin' for a peace pow-wow," Buchanan said testily. "Let's ride to town."

"Don't pick on me. 'Tain't my doin's," said Coco. "People is people, which means they're critters."

"Uh-huh. There's a couple more farms twixt here and town. Let's try."

Coco shook his head. "That man sounded like he knowed."

"Uh-huh," said Buchanan. He squinted at the declining sun. "Tell you what. Might be I won't get to Casey's for supper. So you ride on in and tell 'em not to wait on me."

"You sure you be safe without me?" Coco snickered.

"I'm sure you're mighty contrary all of a sudden." He slapped the withers of Coco's horse and watched it buck, then settle down and run toward home. Buchanan turned and rode up a small hill. The light was still good. He unlimbered his field glasses and peered through them.

There were three riders he could not recognize. One detached himself from the others and rode a little way toward him. It was one of the gunmen of Cross Bar. He thought he recognized the man as McGee by his build.

The rider turned back. Buchanan went to the low plain and rode. He came to more farms. He talked but got only head shakes and shoulder hunching.

He rode into Sheridan and tied up at Bascomb's. The barkeeper batted his eyes but was not unfriendly. Buchanan ordered whiskey, leaned an elbow on the bar and said, "Tell me somethin'. Is there any law around here?"

Bascomb said, "He's comin' through the door right now."

The newcomer was about fifty years of age. He wore city clothing and low-heeled boots and a sharply creased Stetson. His gray mustache was luxuriant. He said,

"Howdy, Buchanan. Heard you were hereabouts. Takin' up with sheep, I hear."

"Arizona, how you been? Have a smile."

"Don't mind if I do." He poured from the bottle, nodded at Bascomb, accepted a beer chaser. The veins in his nose told the story of too many such libations.

"So you're the marshal," said Buchanan.

"Constable." Arizona coughed. "Sheriff ain't never around, so they gave me the job."

"Long way from Abilene."

"Damn few of us left that mind Abilene. Wyatt's still around, doin' what he does."

"Wyatt's a careful man."

"All them Earps—hell, you know 'em."

"Good and bad. Like most of us. I don't suppose you got much to do with the Caseys."

"The sheep people? I know 'em. Kinda simple, ain't they?"

"They don't know the country real good, if that's what you mean."

"Right." Arizona swallowed his whiskey, took a slug of beer. "Now, Jake, he's another kettle o' fish."

"Uh-huh." Buchanan waited.

"He don't bother me none personal. But his people. They come in here, raise hell. I can't draw on a McGee nor a Semple. You mind them boys."

"I mind 'em."

Arizona reached for the bottle. "Put this one on my bill, Bascomb." His eyes were bloodshot. "Was a time."

"You were good."

"Wouldn't be here if I warn't."

It was a hard thing, Buchanan thought, to grow old in the law business. A backwater little burg like Sheridan should have been a haven for Arizona—his real name was Jim Wetherby, from Tucson originally. The presence of Jake's gunmen had made the difference. In his day Arizona would have run them out of town. Back then he had been a better lawman than any of the Earps. He had backed down Wild Bill in Abilene, Buchanan remembered. He had been one of the best.

Bascomb said, "Ain't nothin' anybody around here can do with Robertson's men. It's like they own the town."

"So it seems," said Buchanan.

"You still got that little black lamb?" the bar owner asked.

"Uh-huh."

Arizona said, "I'm plumb ashamed I wasn't here when the mustard was hot."

"Just as well," said Buchanan. "Just a bit o' head knockin'."

"Still and all."

The sun had gone down. Bascomb went around the saloon lighting the kerosene lamps. Buchanan felt the pangs of hunger.

"Any place in town to grab some grub?" he asked.

"Miz Agar, down the street," said Arizona. "Just about to mosey down there myself. Come along."

Buchanan paid for the drinks. "Home cookin'?"

"Good enough."

They went out into the dusk of the evening, Arizona in the lead. As they rounded the corner of the building, an elbow shot out, doubling him over. It belonged to Cobber, the blacksmith from the Cross Bar.

Arizona fell against the building, and Buchanan stepped past him. He saw McGee across the street. There had been three horsemen out on the plain. He did not have time to look for the third.

Cobber was reaching a long arm for Buchanan's throat. He ducked away. He could be amazingly quick for a man of his size and weight. Cobber pursued him.

It would have been easy to draw and shoot. Buchanan did not do so. He whipped a quick left to Cobber's jaw and again moved. Cobber staggered but came on. He was roaring like a bull. Something glinted in his right hand. A beam of light shining through the open door of Bascomb's revealed it to be a chunk of metal.

Now Buchanan did not hesitate. He balanced on his left leg and kicked out with his right. He caught the smithy in the crotch. The big man howled shrilly. Buchanan deftly struck at his thick neck, once, twice, three times. The sound died to a choking noise. Buchanan put both fists together and brought them down hard at the nape of Cobber's neck. At the same time he lifted a knee.

Cobber's nose burst with a splat as his face hit the knee. Buchanan dropped a right cross at the base of the big man's jaw. Cobber was silent then, falling sideways across Bascomb's threshold. He lay like a huge sack of grain.

Arizona said, "Crossfire, Tom."

Buchanan dropped to his knee. His right hand made the grand gesture of a master magician. His gun came out spitting fire and lead. He felt a burning across his left shoulder. He was slow turning around.

Gunfire crackled, the smell of powder was acrid on the air. Arizona said again, "Crossfire!"

McGee was down. Buchanan had found him first, knowing his position, suspecting the plot. Arizona staggered, firing a shot from the hip, cursing himself even as he fell against the building.

Buchanan sought the third man. A spout of flame gutted from behind a horse trough showed him the place. Frantic for fear that Nightshade, tied up nearby, would be hit, he sent two more bullets into the early dark. Then he ran for a vantage point, found it alongside Bascomb's place.

The third man showed an elbow. Buchanan fired from the hip. There was a scream of pain. He ran forward. Semple was sitting behind the trough, his right arm cradled in his left hand, his revolver discarded. Buchanan kicked the firearm away and looked down.

"Last time you'll ever bushwhack a man," he said. "You dirty, rotten bastid, you're a disgrace to your own kind. A backshooter. Hell and high water, Semple, you ought to be hung for this one."

Through the excruciating pain, Semple said, "Might's well be. Goddam you. Might's well be."

Buchanan turned abruptly away. Bascomb was bending over Arizona. A short man with a black bag was running toward them. There was always a country doctor on the scene, Buchanan thought. They had a way of being wherever there were gunshot wounds. This one was bewhiskered and middle-aged.

Buchanan said, "Take care of Arizona. Let the other sonsabitches suffer."

Bascomb said, "McGee don't need no doc."

Cobber was recovering consciousness. Buchanan went to him. He kicked hard. He said, "Get your ass up, you hunk of blubber. Go back to Jake and tell him I'll be askin' questions. Tell him to forget about McGee and Semple. Tell him I aim to be around. Get that straight: I aim to be around."

Cobber gulped. He looked at the body of McGee. He could hear Semple moaning. His eyes grew big as saucers. He wobbled off into the gathering dark to wherever the Cross Bar men had left their horses. For the present, at least, all fight had gone from him.

The gunmen had set it up, Buchanan knew. Cobber had wanted a return fight; they had promised it to him. The odds were he knew nothing about their plan to ambush him. He also doubted that Jake Robertson had knowledge of any of it.

The doctor was working an Arizona. There was blood on the boardwalk, too much of it. Buchanan knelt.

Arizona said, "See?. . . Too damn . . . slow."

"Quick enough to save my buttons," Buchanan said.

"You did good. It was Semple got me."

"Me too." He was aware of the sting of a wound in his shoulder. "Guess none of us is as smart as we used to be."

The doctor said, "Easy, now. I'm going to have to get Arizona to my office."

People were gathering now, citizens frightened but curious. Two men found a shutter in the alley alongside the saloon. They hoisted Arizona aboard and carried him away.

The doctor said to Buchanan, "Name of Abrams. What have you got there?"

"Nothin' much. I can still walk."

They went into the saloon. Semple was calling for help. People walked around him, staring, not even offering sympathy. Cross Bar men had done nothing to make themselves popular in Sheridan.

Dr. Abrams removed Buchanan's shirt with gentle hands. Bascomb brought the whiskey bottle. The medico took it and poured it on the red welt along Buchanan's left shoulder.

"Never touched the bone," he said. "Congratulations." He had a clean roll of linen in his bag. "Now you can drink some of the salve."

Buchanan uptilted the bottle. "The jasper behind the watering trough should be in jail."

"Arizona won't be taking care of the so-called jail," said the doctor. "Not for a while. Maybe never."

"That bad?"

"He may have a piece of lead in his lung."

"God forbid. He saved my life."

"God doesn't take such things into consideration, I've found," said Dr. Abrams wryly. "I'll look at the one that's weeping out there."

"He's got cause to howl," Buchanan said. "Man like him is no use with one arm."

"You sure about the arm?"

"You'll be amputatin'," Buchanan promised.

"His gun arm?"

"Uh-huh."

"Good!" The doctor bustled off.

Buchanan leaned against the bar. Bascomb poured another four ounces, said, "That was damn good work. That'll put a spike in 'em."

"Don't you ever believe it," said Buchanan. "There's plenty more where they came from."

Bascomb made a face. "Never thought of that. Dave Dare and his men, they're just hired hands. Gunslingers, that's different."

"They're for hire. I'll be seein' Jake," said Buchanan. "But hell, it looks damn like a war."

He stared moodily into his liquor. McGee and Semple could be replaced if Jake wanted. His arm ached but he knew what he had to do. He asked directions to the eating place and walked Nightshade down the street.

The town was too small and new to have picked up the stink of cities. Somewhere a guitar sent forth melancholy chords. There was little light, but the stars were kind. A dead man was being carried away to be buried, and perhaps the fray had inaugurated a Boot Hill in Sheridan. It was no good to think of the dead man. Arizona was the one who counted.

The eating place was a small building well-lighted with wall lamps. Buchanan tied up Nightshade to the hitching rail, promising oats for later.

Susan Casey came like a ghost from the shadows. She said in a small voice that he had not heard before, "Buchanan. I need to talk to you."

He was startled. "What are you doin' here?"

She came close to him. "I was riding, thinking. About everything. How it is and how it would be. I followed you to town—not really followed, saw you heading this way."

"You saw what happened?"

She shuddered. "I saw it."

"It ain't pretty, that kinda thing." He took her arm and

steered her toward the restaurant. "Maybe we better eat. It helps to eat."

She said, "I never saw anything like that. I never realized. I've been talkin' about a fight. When you don't know how it is, you can talk big."

The eatery was small but neat. There was a man and a woman; their names were Bert and Elsa Agar. They were silent, dour people. They knew Susan but were not friendly. They were, Buchanan saw, the ordinary citizens, the marginal people, those who dared not take sides. He ordered steaks and whatever the house afforded, and the Agars retired to the kitchen.

Susan was pale beneath her tan. "The . . . fury of it. How quick it happens. The blood, the pain, that man screaming."

"People hurt enough, they holler." He was surprised that she was affected in this manner.

She said, "You're hurt."

"Not the first time. Not much."

"Maybe I'm wrong. Maybe I should listen to Papa. Maybe we should pull out." There were tears in her eyes.

Buchanan said, "You're scared."

"No. Not scared. Not really scared." Color returned to her cheeks. Her eyes were bright. "I think I could fight. If I had to. It's just that—I don't know. I felt sick. But I was excited."

"You mean that's what's worryin' you? That you got excited?"

"Maybe. Maybe it's both." She twisted her strong hands. "Is it because this was the first time?"

He leaned back, easing his shoulder. The pain was steady now, more of an ache. It was nothing unusual to him. "Uh-huh," he said. "It's like anything new. I mind when I was a button comin' up the trail. Two jaspers got into it one night." Time rolled back and he saw himself, a raw kid, eyes wide, watching it. "They had knives. They went

71

around and around the fire. Nobody tried to stop 'em. They cut and slashed. They were big, tough cowboys. They were fightin' over a gal back in El Paso. A no-good gal. When the blood came I got sick. I had to go and throw up.''

"Yes. I did that tonight."

"Then a time later one of the boys jumped me. I done somethin' wrong and he came at me. He had a brandin' iron. It gets tetchy on the trail, and he was a mean one anyway."

"Were you scared?"

He took his time answering. "I was some scared. I was some mad. Somethin' happens, I dunno. You just do what you got to do."

"What you got to do." She nodded. Her voice had returned to normal. "Yes . . . And what did you do?"

"Took away the iron and beat on him."

She repeated, "What you got to do. Buchanan, I just can't give up the land, the sheep, our lives. It would be wrong."

"Uh-huh."

"If we had a chance."

"There's little chance," he said gently.

"There was little chance for you, back there."

"Arizona saved my bacon."

"Could you save us?"

He shook his head. "No way of tellin'. People think the truth'll prevail and all of that. It ain't always so. Jake Robertson, he has his ways. He believes in 'em. It's depending on what can be done about Jake."

She looked straight into his eyes. "You're goin' to stay."

"You think so."

"You're goin' to stay because you like us and because you can't let us go down."

He said, "Mebbe."

"Truly."

He touched his sore shoulder with his right hand. "You're a very smart girl."

"They hurt you and you killed one of them and crippled the other. The big man, he don't count much. It was the gunslingers that made you angry."

He said, "Uh-huh. On t'other hand, they're done for."

"Robertson will bring in more of 'em. You said so."

"Uh-huh."

"And you'll stay and see what happens." She was exultant. "If you stay I can fight. Papa is no coward. Mama is brave."

"And you got Peter Wolf."

She gestured. "Peter is a fighter." He was dismissed in the phrase, Buchanan saw. "Coco . . . Indian Joe, Gowdy."

"A small crew against Cross Bar."

"Then there's you."

The man brought the steaks, potatoes, gravy, corn and hot bread. When he had gone back to the kitchen, Buchanan grinned at the girl.

"Uh-huh. You savvy. A man can't run."

She reached across the table and touched him. Her eyes glowed in the lamplight. Without further words they attacked the hot meal.

FIVE

JOHNNYBEAR RAN EASILY IN THE EARLY DAWN. HE did not know the exact number of miles he had covered, but he knew he was close to the encampment. It had to be in the clearing; there was no other strategic place for Walking Elk and the other Crow. He toed in, relaxed in the manner of his blood kin, his mind moving as easily as his body. He was duty-bound.

He deliberately stepped upon dead wood, making a noise as he came to where they slept in their blankets. They started up, seizing weapons. He called out to them in their language.

Walking Elk stared at him, then prodded the banked fire. "What brings you here, boy with no name?"

"News." His breath was a bit short. He breathed deeply to steady his speech.

"There can be no good news." They were all awake now and listening.

"Buchanan has killed the gunman McGee and crippled the other. The man called Arizona is wounded."

"And what is that to us?"

Johnnybear was confused. "Don't you see? Buchanan is a good man. He is friend to the Caseys. They are the good people who have fed me and clothed me since I was sick that time."

"And you are a white Indian. Peter Wolf is a half-breed; that is his curse. But you—you choose to live with whites."

"Is that wrong?"

"Your great friends the Caseys live on land belonging to the Crow."

"There was a treaty. . . ."

"The treaty was forced upon our fathers with guns. We deny the treaty. The land was ours for hundreds of moons. Thousands of moons." Walking Elk grew emotional. "It is all told about the campfires. Even the old men talk of it. They do nothing, but still they tell the tales."

"I know," said Johnnybear. "I heard the stories when I was a little boy. But when the sickness came no one could cure me. The Caseys took me to the white doctor."

"The medicine men were powerless because the Great Spirit frowned upon us," said Walking Elk. "It is now our duty to stand up so that the Great Spirit will look kindly upon us again."

"I do not know these things," said Johnnybear disconsolately. "I know only that the Caseys mean no harm and that the cattle people will destroy them."

"That is good. Let them kill each other. When they have weakened themselves we will strike."

"Then they will bring in the troops. Nobody wants to see the bluecoats again."

"We will do to them what Crazy Horse and Sitting Bull did at the Big Horn."

Johnnybear's shoulders slumped. He almost said that the Sioux and Cheyenne had been numerous, had been prepared, had taken advantage of mistakes by Yellow Hair, the general. These things he had learned from listening to the talk of white people. He must not repeat them to Walking Elk.

He said only, "You would do well to take sides with the sheep people against the cattle kings."

"We take the side of no whites," said Walking Elk. "We will steal their guns and their sheep and their cattle until we grow strong. Others will join us. We will drive out the white eyes."

Johnnybear said, "May I now go in peace?"

"You are Crow. You could help us by bringing information. Their weaknesses. Their plans."

"Yes," said Johnnybear. "I could do that."

He lifted a hand and turned and trotted toward the Casey ranch. It had been worth a try, he thought. Help must come from someplace or the Caseys would perish. He would, of course, die with them.

He now saw that Walking Elk was seized with a dream that could never come true. Johnnybear had learned a lot by being quiet, unseen, his ears wide open. There could be no aid for his patrons from the Crow, he now knew. The old men were quiet on the reservation. The young men were too few and too intent upon their own wild, hopeless scheme. His heart was leaden as he ran back to his chores.

Cobber nursed his bruises. He had managed to ride back to Cross Bar alone, knowing he had disobeyed orders, fearful of the outcome. Dave Dare and the riders were pulling on their clothes against the chill morning air.

Cobber said, "He's a frightenin' man, Buchanan."

"He's got you buffaloed, all right," said Dave Dare.

Cobber's bunk was larger than the others, in a corner of the long room. He bent painfully, rummaged beneath the cot and came up with a length of bright steel chain of small, elongated links. He ran it through his big hands.

"Run into a black b'ar oncet," he rumbled. "Up in the mountains beyond Denver. Big bugger. Jest for fun I snuck behind it. Got this here around his neck. Choked him t' death."

"Black bear," said Dave Dare. "Buchanan, now. He's more of a grizzly."

Cobber wagged his beard. "The day'll come. By God, the day'll come."

The rider called Bowlegs asked, "What you think the boss'll do now, Dave?"

"I dunno. He was kinda funny about it. Said he warned us all, like. Said he told us not to go near Buchanan."

"Him drunk again, he'll say anything."

"Didn't give a damn about McGee nor Semple. Said let 'em rot. Said they was plain dumb," Cobber said.

"What about them sheep?" Bowlegs asked.

"Said leave everything be till Buchanan leaves," Dare told him.

"What if Buchanan don't pull stakes?"

"I dunno," said Dare testily. "I just take orders. And I obey 'em. That's why we're alive."

After a moment Bowlegs said, "Y' know, Cross Bar don't need nothin' more'n we got. Them sheep are trouble, sartain. But they ain't that much trouble."

"It's up to the boss," Dave reiterated. "This here's a good place to work, 'ceptin' for winters. It's up to Jake."

"And his gal."

"Now, you hush up on her."

"C'mon, Dave. You know she's been seein' that half-breed out on the range. We all seen her waylayin' him."

Dave Dare grabbed the smaller man by the shirt. "By geez, you keep your mouth off her or you draw your pay. You understand what I'm sayin'?"

Bowlegs squirmed away. "All right, Dave. All right."

The other riders averted their faces, busying themselves with small, useless tasks. Dave Dare knew. They all knew.

All but Bowlegs also knew enough to keep their knowledge to themselves.

In the main house Jake Robertson poured whiskey for himself and Mrs. Bacon. Claire watched, resigned.

Robertson said, "I done told them."

"We know," said Claire. "They went in to kill Buchanan. You warned them. One dead, one crippled, one beaten. Now what do you propose?"

He drank. "Gotta bring in bigger and better guns."

"To kill Buchanan and the Caseys?"

"Hush such talk," said the housekeeper. She reached out and touched Jake's hand. "Your pa ain't out to hurt people. Just to get rid of them damned sheep."

"To do that people must be killed." Claire's chin came out hard and strong. "It is no good, Papa. No good."

"Protection. They got Buchanan. He already killed McGee, didn't he?" His speech was slightly slurred, his eyes unfocused. "You been to school too much, baby. You don't know what it takes to hold on to what you got."

He finished his drink. Mrs. Bacon followed suit and trotted to the sideboard to pour another for each of them. Claire watched, smoldering. Mrs. Bacon had been speaking up more and more as days went by. There was an Irish girl, an immigrant, in the kitchen now and a boy to help her. Mrs. Bacon was beginning to rule the household.

Claire said, "You don't need to fight to hold what you have. You're a rich man. You could sell out and we could travel the world."

Her father snorted. "Who wants to see the world? My world's right here. Yessir. On'y place I'd wanta see would be mebbe back home in Texas. The world can go to hell."

Claire said, "I would like to see the world."

"You can take a journey any ol' time you want. Do you good. Getcha outa here."

"Wouldn't that be nice?" said Mrs. Bacon, beaming. "You could go any ol' place you wanted."

78

Claire arose and went to the sideboard. She picked up two bottles of whiskey. She stared hard at her papa and Mrs. Bacon, then went into the kitchen. She emptied the bottles into the sink. Then she went upstairs to her room. She undressed, donned a robe and sat in a chair beside an oil lamp. She rocked back and forth, her mind going around and around. There was no sign of her dimples. Her knuckles were white. Her eyes were dark blue, her chin hard.

She thought of Peter Wolf, his straight, hard body, his black gaze . . . his indifference to her. She thought of Susan Casey. Claire knew she was in love with Peter Wolf, who was, she could plainly see, in love with Susan.

She could hear her father roaring her name downstairs because of the whiskey. That's all he would do, holler and complain. Mrs. Bacon would agree and suggest punishment and then Jake would turn on Mrs. Bacon and tell her to mind her own business and then they would open another bottle. It was all part of a scene that had become dismal.

She considered Susan. She could not hate the girl. If she knew anything, she knew hatred was destructive. She had temperament of her own; she recognized strength in others. The Caseys were good people.

Then there was Buchanan. In him she saw the epitome of a dying breed. The frontier still existed; she was a part of it despite her schooling, her appreciation of other values. Buchanan stood for what the West believed in, would suffer for, would die for. She saw it all clearly.

She found no comfort in her clear vision. It was not a time for women in the West. So long as Jake Robertson was alive she would be his daughter and that only. She could only sit back and wait.

She could, however, ride out and hope to see Peter Wolf.

A lamp in the Casey stable threw long black shadows. Nightshade moved restlessly in his stall. Buchanan and

Coco knelt beside the little black lamb. Susan hovered, uncertain.

She said, "Maybe he's got a fever."

"He's real peaked," said Coco.

Johnnybear came with hot water. No one knew exactly what to do with it.

"He won't eat," said Buchanan. "His belly's swole some."

Coco brought a horse blanket. "Keep him warm. That's what you do with babies, ain't it?"

"I never had a baby," Susan said.

"I got some of that medicine the Crow gave us the recipe for," said Coco.

"That's for humans," Buchanan said.

"Heap big medicine," said Johnnybear.

"It's mainly for bullet holes." Buchanan was wearing a poultice of the cure-all the Crow girl had given them at the time of the siege. Its healing power was nothing short of miraculous. "Where on the little critter would we put it?"

They all furrowed their brows. The black lamb blatted his complaint faintly.

Coco said, "He brought us here, he did. That's how we all come together. Got to take care of him no matter what."

They all looked to Buchanan. At a total loss, he felt the nose of the lamb. "With a dog if he's got a cold nose, he's okay. Hot nose he ain't feelin' good."

"So?" asked Susan.

"Seems neither one to me." He rocked back on his heels. His shoulder burned. His left arm was stiff and sore. "Be doggone if I know what to do."

Beth Bower said from the door, "Goodness sakes, you folks. Just get out of the way, please."

She had a bottle in her hand. The light was kind to her bright hair; her violet eyes were amused. She had a truly wonderful gait, Buchanan thought, a fine figure of a woman. She was about thirty, he thought, young to be a widow and alone in this land. She went to the lamb, tilted its head.

She said, "If one of you is strong enough to pry open its jaws . . . ?"

Buchanan obeyed. She uncorked the bottle. She poured carefully, without spilling a drop. The lamb choked a bit, then allowed the thick liquid to slip down his throat.

Beth Bower stood up. "Now you-all better go about your business, 'ceptin' Johnnybear. He'll have to do the dirty work, I'm afraid."

"What's that you gave it?" asked Coco.

"Why, castor oil, of course. Anybody with half an eye could see what ails the critter. Shoo! Inside!"

They went meekly, following her. The elder Caseys were having a drink in the parlor. They smiled at the trio of would-be nurses. Casey said, "Beth knows about as much as a doctor. She's been invaluable to us."

"Nursed me through a bad spell not too long ago," Mrs. Casey added. "Took care of Susan's sprained ankle. Let's all have a drink, shall we?"

They chatted. Susan went to the piano. Peter Wolf was missing, Buchanan noted.

The music was soothing. It was a most pleasant domestic scene, one in which Buchanan seldom found himself. Coco, nursing a glass of milk in a corner, obviously reveled in it. The threat of tremendous trouble ahead seemed to have failed to touch these people, Buchanan thought.

Yet he caught Susan's glances from time to time. She did not play the gay tunes. Her fingers were nimble, but the music was tender, sometimes sober. She had seen the violence erupt; she had seen the consequences.

Now that he was committed, Buchanan knew he must forthwith count the chances, the odds. He had no doubt that Jake would send for reinforcements, probably had already done so. There was no lack of guns for hire. The coming of law in highly populated areas had driven them all to the roads. Jake had money; they needed money. It was as simple as that.

Buchanan had friends, dozens of them. One of the reasons he kept them, he reminded himself, was that he never called upon them to put their lives on the line. He might bring them in by sending a telegram to Billy Button in New Mexico. He smiled to himself, knowing what the headstrong Billy would think if he were asked to come and fight for sheep people. Billy ran a big ranch on the high plain, fine Herefords and longhorns mixed with newly acquired Angus for crossbreeding. Billy and his wife and son, Tommy, were all the family Buchanan had. There was no way he would disturb their current peace and quiet.

He wondered if he dared hope that there was a chance to get Jake Robertson to talk bobwire. He doubted it down to his boots. Still, he could try. There was the girl; he had seen something in her that he admired.

The music broke off. Susan said, "I don't feel much like playing tonight. I can't help thinking of poor Arizona."

"He's a tough old brother," said Buchanan.

"That other man, the one tried to kill you. He'll lose his arm, won't he?"

"So said the doctor."

"For wages," she mused. "They know they must fight with guns sooner or later. For money."

"For hire. It's a bit different," Buchanan said. "They ain't assassins. They hope to hold the shootin' down through their reputations. They got their pride. That's why they come for me."

Coco added, "It's always the same. We get to a place, we do somethin' or other. Then they come for Tom."

"The luck of the game." Buchanan dissembled; he was uneasy at being thought the savior of the West. He was not; he never had been. Time, tide and circumstance had presented situations. He was thrust into them. He did what he thought was right. That was all.

"Let us speak of other matters," said Shawn Casey, ever discerning, sensing Buchanan's discomfort.

Two men held Semple. The smell of whiskey was strong in the small room where he lay stretched on Dr. Abrams's operating table. There were clamps for his legs, but his right arm lay free. He was stripped to the waist, his mouth in a ghastly grin. Bascomb stood by, bottle in hand.

Semple said, "For God's sake, git on with it, Doc." His voice was high, his speech slurred. "I can't swalley much more booze, damn it."

"Sorry I don't have ether, son," said the doctor. "It's in small supply. Had a sheepherder in here . . ."

"The hell with your goddam sheepherder. Saw the damn thing off. It's killin' me."

"Patience . . . patience."

The thin-bladed surgical saw was bright and clean. Semple stared at it, bleary-eyed. One of the men holding him swallowed hard and turned pale. Bascomb put down the bottle and shoved the man aside.

"I got a strong stomach, Jeb. Lemme handle this."

"Somebody damn well better do somethin'," howled Semple.

The doctor said, "In the next room I have a good man in serious condition due to you fellows. If I don't handle this surgery properly, you might be in worse shape. So kindly shut up."

Bascomb said, "Let's get it over with, eh, Doc?"

The man named Jeb leaned against the wall. "Makes us all sick, Doc, waitin' around."

Oblivious, the doctor went on, "All during the war we lost patients because of pyemia or gangrene. Terrible. Then Dr. Lister discovered the method we know now, which reduces the danger . . ." His saw touched flesh and Semple screamed. No one heard the end of Dr. Abrams's little lecture.

In the next room the doctor's wife wiped Arizona's lips and smiled at him. She was a plain, patient woman with graying hair. "Pay no attention. He's operating on the man who shot you."

"I wouldn't wish that on a dog," whispered Arizona. He was having trouble with his breath. He shut his mouth tight. There had been other wounds, injuries of all kinds. The frontier was rough and he had been a ranch hand before he was a marshal. There had been great days and bad days and this, he thought, might well be the end. He managed a smile to comfort the woman who was being kind to him.

The tough Texas buggy rattled on the uneven trail between Cross Bar and Sheridan. Mrs. Bacon handled the reins. Jake Robertson nursed a bottle and talked incessantly every yard of the way. The stars shone on the land, lighting the trail. In the distance a working dog barked at a strayed sheep.

"Nobody understands," Jake said, " 'Ceptin' mebbe you. My daughter, she's into all them newfangled ideas. Peace. That's all she talks about. Peace with sheepmen. Peace with Injuns. Peace with every dumb soul in the world. Is that the way I got where I am?"

"No, Jake." The front wheel struck a dip and she was thrown against him. "Just take it easy now, Jake."

"I told them fools not to go agin Buchanan, didn't I?"

"You sure did, Jake," she said soothingly, liking the contact with his heavy body. "Their own fault they got in trouble."

"Buchanan, he was a friend, I thought. Not that I blame him for what happened. What I can't abide is him sidin' with the sheep people. I thought he might go on his way. He won't, not now. The boys went agin him, and I know his pride. He's a Texan for all his New Mexico talk. The Lord knows I don't wanta fight him. But a man's got to stand up for his rights. I brought all them cows to Wyoming and I'm goin' to keep 'em here and no bobwire and to hell with sheep.''

"You got every right.''

"Dave and them, they're dumb, but they're all right. Good cattlemen. They earn their pay. Ain't tough enough. Oh, they'll fight if they have to. Need better guns.''

She said, "If you think so, Jake.''

"Damn Cobber, tryin' to fight Buchanan with bare hands. McGee and Semple, now, they had the right notion even if it didn't work for 'em. You got to take Buchanan by surprise. Not that I'd have anything to do with a bushwhack,'' he added hastily. "Not my style, not at all.''

"I know. You're an honest man.''

"I hope to God. I pay my way. I bought the damn sheriff. He won't bother none with Sheridan. I know the governor of Wyoming well enough. Leastways I think so—never trust a politician. What I got to do is protect what I own.''

"You sure do, Jake.'' She drove into the town. It was pitch-dark, but a light burned in Dr. Abrams's hospital and before the post office–telegraph office. "Where you want to go?''

He said, "Tie up at Doc's. I'll have a look.''

She obeyed. He tipped the bottle, swallowing then coughing. She took the whiskey and sipped herself. With an effort he managed to step down. Then he stumbled.

She said, "Jake! Be careful. I swear, you come in here without a gun and guzzlin' liquor and . . .''

"Hush up, woman. I'm like Buchanan thataway. Only carry a weapon when you mean to use it.'' He laughed. "You comin'?''

She crawled down and they went arm in arm to the door. Mrs. Abrams opened it, wan with exhaustion. She said, "I thought you might be stopping by.''

"Yes, ma'am.'' Jake removed his hat. "My man. Is he alive?''

"He is.''

"Like to see him, ma'am."

Mrs. Abrams said, "This way, please."

She led him to where Semple lay, the stump bandaged, his eyes closed. The odor of antiseptic was strong. Mrs. Bacon said, "Lordy, he does look beat."

Dr. Abrams came from the next room. "Mr. Robertson, you might come with me."

Jake said, "Why, sure. Anything I can do." He fumbled in his pocket, took out money. "I'm payin' all bills."

Dr. Abrams was silent, leading the way. Jake stopped dead in his tracks. Arizona lay with his hands across his chest, coins upon his eyelids, a tight little smile on his lips.

"Christ!" said Jake. "I didn't know."

"Your money won't bring him back. It won't replace the arm of your man in there, who probably killed him."

Jake said, "Now look, Doc. I didn't have anything to do with this."

"The men who attacked Buchanan work for you."

"They was goin' against my strict orders. I got proof."

"You may need it."

Jake began to back out of the room. "Semple . . . he'll be held for the circuit court, then?"

"If I have anything to do with it. If I can find your sheriff."

"Now, Doc . . . I'll see the sheriff is notified. Right's right. Arizona, he was a good man."

"You couldn't buy him," said Dr. Abrams coldly.

"Now . . . now . . ." Jake put money on the operating table. He said, "All right. It was wrong. They done wrong."

Mrs. Bacon was staring at him. She took his arm as they went outdoors. The street was silent. She walked him to the carriage.

"I never seen you like this," she said in a small voice.

"I never been like this." He reached into the buggy for

the whiskey, drank deeply emptying it, then stared at the bottle, shook his head. "Now we're in for it."

"Like you said, you didn't tell them—"

He cut her off. "Arizona saved Buchanan's life. Don't you know what that means?"

"Well . . ."

"Buchanan will never leave here until Semple goes to trial. That could be a month, two months. You know how slow the judge is makin' his rounds."

"Buchanan would believe you if you told him it was against your orders."

"Makes no never mind. Arizona is dead."

"Can't you do somethin'?"

With a visible effort, he pulled himself together. He gestured and she followed him down the street. The post office and the telegraph station were in the same building. Jake rapped on the door. A light came on, a voice called, "Closed for the night, damn it."

"Jake Robertson here. Open up."

The door opened up a crack. "Mr. Robertson? What's wrong?"

Jake pushed his way inside. "Every damn thing." He produced more money, threw it down. "You, Simpson, you know me. I want to send a telegram. Right now."

"Well, sure." Simpson was a skinny man with a scrawny beard. "If it's that important." He slid the money into a drawer without counting it. "Anything you say."

Jake said, "What's more, I don't want another soul to know about it. You understand?"

"Sure, Mr. Robertson." He scurried to his key. "You want to write it down or just tell me?"

"No writin'." He thought a moment, wishing he had another drink. He put his hands to his head and began talking.

"To Fritz Wilder . . . care of Delaney's Saloon, Casper, Wyoming . . . Hell, you know Casper's in Wyoming . . . To Fritz Wilder . . . Need half-dozen your men . . . Soon as possible . . . Top pay like always . . . Don't answer this . . . Get here . . . Sign it 'Jake.' Just 'Jake.' Understand?''

"The stage from Casper will be through day after tomorrow."

"I know all about that. Damn it, send the message."

Simpson's hand tapped the key. Jake listened until the last echo died sharply in the room. Then he said, "One word outa you and Fritz will come for you, too."

"You know me, Mr. Robertson. I ain't never let you down yet, now, have I?"

"Just so it ain't the first time." He was staggering now as he went to the buggy. He clambered in with some difficulty. The woman turned the horse around and headed for Cross Bar.

Jake muttered, "This ain't a good thing. This is a damn bad thing. Buchanan, he's a good man. Why in tarnation hell did he have to come here at this time?"

She said, "There's a bad time for everything, Jake."

"And a good time, damn it."

"Lots of good times. The bad times come and go. Man like you, he makes the good times come."

He wanted to believe it. He slumped in the seat. His mind was clear enough. He saw things he did not want to see. He heard sounds he hated to hear. He would have preferred to sleep, but sleep would not come to him, not even when he was home and in Mrs. Bacon's bed.

SIX

FOR TWO DAYS BUCHANAN RODE THE PLAIN, SOME-
times with Coco, sometimes with Shawn Casey. He learned
to appreciate the border collies and the McNabs, the work
dogs who were gentle when need be and fierce if necessary.
Because of the dogs, Casey explained, fewer herders were
needed. Without the dogs it would have been impossible to
control the herds.

Of the men engaged in herding, only Gowdy and Indian
Joe seemed to be fighters. There was a Mexican, Manuel
Cordova, who had pride and whose dogs were fighters at his
command. He had no stomach for guns, he told Buchanan,
nor did any of the other Casey employees.

However, for these two days there was peace. The sun
shone; clouds made many-storied palaces floating high in
the blue sky. All was calm.

On the third day Susan and Peter Wolf and Shawn Casey
gathered at noon upon the handy hilltop that Buchanan had
used for an observation post. The sheep browsed, and far

away the cattle of Cross Bar were somnolent, bunched near the big house. Six men came riding from Sheridan, traversing the rough trail to the ranch. Buchanan unlimbered his field glasses.

His jaw hardened. He said, "Fritz Wilder. I'd know him anywhere, anytime."

"Wilder?" asked Casey.

"The wildest. A boss gunslinger. Fast and mean."

"Six of them to replace Semple and McGee," said Susan. "And Miss Priss talked about peace and good will."

Buchanan said mildly, "I wouldn't reckon Claire had anything to do with it."

"They're here," she retorted.

Peter Wolf said, "They're here to wipe us out." He had his rifle half out of the scabbard when Buchanan stopped him. "Better now than later."

Shawn Casey said, "No, Peter. We can't do that, you know."

Buchanan returned to his field glasses. "Uh-huh. Shawn's right. And looky yonder."

He handed the glasses to Susan. She squinted and then said, "Robertson's buggy. She's drivin'. Miss Priss."

"So we'll talk."

"I won't believe a word," said Susan.

Peter Wolf was silent, uneasy. Shawn Casey was hopeful. Buchanan waited, hoping for the best, fearing the worst. Fritz Wilder was evil; he was without compunction. Men who rode with him did his bidding or suffered grave consequences. It could be that Robertson wanted the gunslingers as a threat, a bulwark behind which he could command without resorting to violence. It could be that the owner of Cross Bar was about to deliver an ultimatum.

The riders below reined in. The carriage stopped and Robertson talked to the horsemen. Claire sat straight and aloof during the conversation, Buchanan noted. He was certain that he had been right about the girl. Now, if only Peter Wolf would make his manners . . . He put the thought aside. Peter had eyes only for Susan Casey.

Fritz Wilder and his men rode on toward Cross Bar and were soon out of sight beyond a ridge of land. Buchanan could see a herd of cattle to the south and sheep to the north. Down below to the west lay the ravine into which the sheep had been driven. It was, he thought, a proper spot for a meeting.

The carriage came slowly up the hill. Buchanan and the others dismounted. Claire tied up the reins to the buggy, and Jake tilted the springs getting to earth, bandy-legged, over-weight, flushed. Claire was wearing a divided skirt and a blouse through which her creamy skin showed. She darted a glance at Peter Wolf, then looked away.

Claire said, "Papa, you haven't met Susan Casey and her father, Mr. Shawn Casey."

"Pleased, I'm sure." Jake did not offer to shake hands. The smell of alcohol was strong on him. "You wanted a meetin'. This here's a good place." He waved a thick arm. "It's all out yonder for everybody to see."

Shawn Casey said, "Room enough for everybody."

"If everybody will agree," Buchanan said.

Jake glared at him. "You talk like you own some part of it. It ain't yours to palaver about."

"Uh-huh," said Buchanan. "On t'other hand, seems like you and your people sorta put me into it."

"Please," said Claire. "Can't we talk about peace among us?"

Shawn Casey said, bowing, "That is my sincere hope."

"Me too," said Jake. He took a piece of paper from his pocket. "Now, this here is a map." He extended it to Casey. "Y' see how I got it figured? That graze I marked is mine. I need every foot of it."

Casey studied the map. "In other words—you need a

hundred miles square. Why, that even covers the Crow reservation.''

''What I need I take. And I hold it.'' He swelled up like a balloon. ''Now, you hear. I offer you ten thousand dollars to build you a new house wherever you go.''

Susan gasped and started forward. Peter Wolf restrained her. Buchanan laughed and everyone stared at him.

Buchanan said, ''I'll give you twenty thousand for your house and stables and all you got here, Jake.''

''You're crazy, man.'' Jake's eyes popped.

''Plenty of graze in Wyoming, Montana. Easy drive for your beef. I don't see anything wrong with the deal.''

Claire said, ''Now, really, Mr. Buchanan.''

''You . . . you are plumb loco,'' stammered Jake.

''Could be. On t'other hand, Fritz Wilder and his guns don't scare me all that much.''

''You done laid out two of my best men. I ain't sayin' you did wrong, the way it happened. But you done it, and I aim to protect myself.''

''Against Mr. and Mrs. Casey and their daughter?''

''And that breed and the Injuns roamin' around.''

Buchanan motioned Peter Wolf to stay still. ''And me?''

''By God and you, too, Buchanan! I knowed you a long time and I know how good you are. But I'm Jake Robertson, and nobody is goin' to stop me from grazin' my cattle.''

Buchanan waved an arm. ''Your cows are eatin' good.''

''I'm bringin' in twice that many. You hear? I'm growin'. I aim to be the biggest cattleman in this here country.''

Buchanan said deliberately, ''That's the booze talkin', Jake. There's outfits like the Powers in Montana would eat you alive. Come down to earth and let's talk sense. Like bobwire.''

''Bobwire!'' Jake became apoplectic. ''Bobwire! Buchanan, with my own hands I'll shoot anybody strings wire.''

''You couldn't hit the side of a barn with a shotgun,'' Buchanan told him bluntly. "You just brought in a half-dozen outlaws. Do you think the governor will stand for it?"

"I know he will! I know my right to defend myself!"

Buchanan shook his head. "You're beatin' a dead horse, Jake. Sober up and think it over."

Claire spoke up suddenly, "Papa doesn't want war. Honest he doesn't. I don't want war." She was staring at Peter Wolf. "Why can't we get together? Be partners. Share and share alike."

Susan snapped, "Trust your father and his killers? Allow our sheep to be run over cliffs?"

Shawn Casey sighed. He handed the map back to Jake. "Mr. Robertson, let me think this over. And you think about it as well. Consider all the elements. The government has leased grazing rights to all of us. Think about that. Perhaps we can talk again."

"There ain't but one thing to talk on. Sheep ruin the grazin' for the cattle. We got our rights and we can handle any little old thing comes up. That's the whole of it." He stalked back to the buggy.

Claire lingered, pleading. "Something can be done. Something must be done."

Susan said, "Maybe you and Peter can figure out something." She started for her horse.

Peter Wolf had turned brick red. Buchanan waved an arm. He said, "Somethin' is bein' done. Look yonder."

Under the bowl of cerulean Wyoming sky all was plainly visible. The Cross Bar riders were gathered, rolling cigarettes, talking. On the far side of the herd of cattle several young men on ponies were working with incredible speed. While Jake hollered to high heaven, they were cutting out a dozen fleet young steers, expertly gathering them, driving them westward.

"Shoot off a gun, damn it!" yelled Jake. "Get them knuckleheads started after 'em."

"Don't have a gun among us," said Buchanan. "This here was a peace meetin', remember?"

"Claire, get in the damn buggy," Jake howled.

"Not me, Papa," said Claire. "It's downhill and risky. Texas buggies turn over too easy."

Jake gathered up the reins and whipped the horse. It was downhill all the way, and the weight of the buggy was not equal to the speed of the animal. In twenty yards the vehicle turned over. Jake bounced loose, rolling over and over. He sat up, waved a fist and began running.

Buchanan said, "By the time he gets there, the Crow on the reservation will be eatin' prime ribs."

"Walking Elk is ridin' today," said Susan. "Now, Miss Robertson, how do you like seeing your stock run off?"

Claire said, "We can spare them. I've heard the Indian agent isn't feeding the Crows well enough."

Susan was baffled. "You do catch on to a lot of things. If only your father could see through a hole in a millstone."

"My father . . . He *is* still my father," said Claire. She looked at Peter Wolf. "Could you give me a lift back to the ranch?"

There was a moment when it seemed he would refuse. Then he coughed and gave her a hand up into his saddle. He did not mount. He led the horse down the hill to Cross Bar.

Susan said, "She sure dotes on him."

"Kinda one-sided," said Buchanan. He was watching the Indians drive the stolen cattle into the woods. His heart was heavy. Jake would never hold still for it, he knew. The Cross Bar riders would go in pursuit. There was really no place for Walking Elk to hide from a determined search. No good would come of it in the end.

Susan was saying, "Maybe it would solve everything if Peter took up with her."

"It could make things ten times worse. To Jake a half-breed is lower than a snake's belly. No, my dear, there's no way out that I can see."

"Except to fight."

"Uh-huh." It was a fight against odds as huge as he had ever faced.

Shawn Casey said, "I'm against fighting. I hate violence. But there does come a time."

Susan started. "You will stay and fight, Father?"

"Ten thousand dollars. That did it. We built that house to live in," Casey said to Buchanan. "It's our home."

"Uh-huh," said Buchanan. "A home." He thought of Billy Button and how it had been necessary to defend the ranch in New Mexico and how they had nearly lost it and what it had meant to them all. "Reckon I know about that."

He brought his field glasses to bear. Walking Elk and his men and the cattle were gone into the woods. The Cross Bar men had awakened as the herd milled and were riding in pursuit. Jake was down to a walk, obstinately making his way to the scene of action.

"Nothin' to do here," said Buchanan. "Might's well go back home and think about whatever."

Whatever wasn't much to bank upon, he thought. They rode under the faultless blue bowl of a sky.

Once into the trees Walking Elk said, "Crazy Bird, you and Eagle Feather cut brush."

They obeyed, tying it to their blanket saddles with braided lariats of their own manufacture. Again they rode hard, finding passages in the forest known only to them, their tracks covered from anyone less astute than the most canny plainsman. Night came and on they went, tireless, to an arroyo wherein grew grass for grazing. There Walking Elk delegated one disconsolate brave to stand as sentinel and keep the cattle from straying.

The tiny stream which trickled into the arroyo had become a small river from the rains. They bathed in it, gleeful, boasting of how they had fooled the white eyes and taken the cattle for meat. Walking Elk donned his clean leggings and shirt and summoned Crazy Bird. "Leave only the guard. We will now go to the old men."

Crazy Bird, second in command, a thoughtful youth, asked, "Is that wise, brother? The old men do not believe as we do."

"We must make them see. They must believe."

"They are blinded by defeat. We know this."

"They are being cheated. The sign will be clear. It is a time to strike while the cowman and the sheepman fight each other."

If Crazy Bird had doubts, this was no time to show them and he knew it. Walking Elk was riding the crest of his triumph, driving now for his ultimate dream. The five braves followed in single file, taking devious routes to the reservation. It was late and the fires were low when they arrived.

They made their way to the main lodge, where a low fire burned within. They were summoned inside. Lone Eagle stood tall, gazing at them, his visage stern.

"So you have returned."

"With good news, my chief," said Walking Elk. "The white eyes are fighting each other. We have taken beef for the warriors. It is safely hidden in the place you know. It is time to arm and strike!"

"Strike." The chieftain seemed to grow taller. "And you have provided meat. For how many? How many rifles have you?"

"We have a hidden store of guns."

"Muskets. Worn-out rifles. Pistols, unsafe. We know what you have stolen, Walking Elk."

"The meat . . ."

"Do you think they will not know it if we have fresh meat not provided by the agent? Do you think they will not be searching? Fool! You could bring us all down. Forget you ever stole the meat!"

"It is the time, I tell you! We will send to our brethren.

They will come with us. Yellow Hair was killed, his men with him. It can be done again!''

"And you will lead them. Yes, you have always wanted that. I have watched you. I have noted with great sadness that you are not of these times.''

"I am of my time!''

"Too little and too late,'' said the chief. "You have never seen the bluecoats ride. You cannot accept the massacres. Even now you could bring the wrath of the white man down upon the women and children and the old people of this tribe.''

"I say we can fight!''

"And be slain.'' A woman moved in the background; a child whimpered. Lone Eagle pointed a long arm. "You will go, Walking Elk. You will find your rainbow, but there will be death at the end. You must not bring that to us. You may depart in peace this time. But do not return until you have seen the error of your ways.''

"I will go. You will live to be sorry. I am sending to the Blackfoot, the Sioux, for help. You shall see.'' He shook a fist. "I am ashamed to be a Crow! There is no longer courage in you.''

He dashed out of the lodge. Crazy Bird followed, shaking his head. They went to their horses.

Crazy Bird said, "Lone Eagle is a wise man. He has fought the bluecoats.''

"He is an old fool!'' said Walking Elk.

"What do we do with the cattle?''

"We fatten it and eat it and perhaps sell it. There are those who will buy and ask no question. We will steal more guns. We will watch the sheepman and the cattleman kill each other.''

"And the man Buchanan?''

Walking Elk mounted. "Let him look to himself. He has chosen to make his stand. We will see what good it comes to—for us.''

After a moment Crazy Bird said, "The man, Buchanan. He was good to the Crow once upon a time."

"He is no better than the others."

"But he is big medicine. Maybe if we helped the sheepman, Buchanan would help us."

"We need no help! Our destiny is to gain back the land that is ours!"

Crazy Bird remained silent. They rode back to the arroyo in the stillness of the countryside.

In the Casey stable Buchanan played with the little black lamb, now nearly well. Coco said, "The Indians steal a half-dozen outa thousands of cattle and Jake goes crazy. People ain't got no sense hardly at all sometimes."

"It's a bad thing," said Buchanan. "It's a scary bad thing."

"They'll go after the Crow, won't they?"

"It's what they'll do when they finally find 'em . . ." said Buchanan. "You know the rule against rustlin'."

"I know Mr. Lynch real good. I seen him operate."

"There's no way to stop 'em."

Susan came to them. "They'll hang an Indian, won't they?"

"If they find 'em."

She said, "More deaths. Tomorrow they bury Arizona."

"And McGee," said Buchanan.

"You had to kill him!" said Susan.

"I'm not apologizin'," Buchanan told her.

"But you're not pleased. Not happy. I know that."

"It never goes down good to kill a man," said Buchanan. It was a subject he thought about a lot but did not discuss.

She said slowly, "Now I know the difference between you and a gunman. He kills for hire."

"Somethin' like that." He was evasive.

"If I were a man, I could kill for a cause," she said defiantly. "If somethin's right, it's worth killin' for."

"Uh-huh," said Buchanan. He went to where Johnnybear was polishing harness. "Don't you ever take up a gun, little man. When you're growed they'll be a thing of the past, I hope."

"If a gun is needed, I'll use one." Johnnybear was solemn. "Walking Elk, he'll be killed by the cowmen, won't he?"

"Accordin' to his luck," said Buchanan. "Accordin' to how the cards fall."

"No guns," said Coco. "Praise be to that day."

"Until then keep your powder dry," said Susan. "Even father is ready to fight now."

Buchanan was silent. The appearance of Fritz Wilder and his men had bitten deep. He had not thought Jake would go so far with such dispatch.

Coco held up his two hard, gnarled fists. "Man was meant to fight with these. Tom, he done both. Guns and hands. And sometimes feet." He chuckled. "Ain't killed nobody yet"—he sobered—" 'Ceptin' with bullets."

Buchanan rubbed his shoulder and said dryly, "Bullets have been known to do things to me."

"That's it," said Susan. "Self-defense. The law of survival."

"Uh-huh," said Buchanan. He returned to the black sheep. Innocence lay there, in its round eyes, its weak little bleat, its helplessness against the world.

From the house, Mrs. Casey called, "Suppertime, please."

The others departed. Buchanan lingered, feeling the silky ears of the lamb. There was a lot to think about, doubts to be banished, plans to be made.

Jake Robertson poured a drink for Fritz Wilder. "Them hands of mine couldn't catch a bull in a corral," he said.

Wilder, dark, handsome, sleek, relaxed, said, "Not

much at following trail myself. Indians are like ghosts when they have reason."

"This here's just a start. They get away with a half-dozen and they'll raid a whole herd some stormy night."

"Could be." Wilder was an enigma, a man of education with no known past. "You should take action."

"I got to."

"Find an Indian. Hang him."

Jake scowled. "Just any ol' Injun? That ain't the way I do business. I want them young-uns been livin' in the woods. Them's the guilty ones."

"Find one, hang one. Give them a lesson, something to think about."

"All I want from you is protection agin Tom Buchanan," said Jake testily.

"Ah, yes. Buchanan. I saw him in action once."

"He's been in plenty action."

"It was in Silver City. There was a woman involved, a whore, mind you. No concern of his, none at all. He is not a man for whores, no more than I." He sipped his drink, stretching his well-tailored legs. "Man was a fast fellow. Name of Eggers. He drew first. Buchanan shot him through the hand. The man drew his left-hand gun. Buchanan killed him with one through the heart. Swiftest moves I ever witnessed."

"Is he faster than you?"

Without changing position Wilder drew his revolver and shot a blossom from the scraggly garden Claire had begun and never finished. He said, "I won't know until we try, now, will I?"

He turned with an easy smile. He looked into the twin barrels of a sawed-off shotgun.

Jake said, "Don't you never shoot off no gun on the premises of my house without warnin'. I might be old and gettin' fat, but I don't kowtow to no two-bit gunslinger."

Wilder bowed his head, still smiling. "I beg your pardon, I truly do. It was thoughtless of me."

"And if it comes to hangin' Injuns, I want 'em to be caught in the act. I know you ain't no cowboy, but you can ride. I'll want you to be lookin' for them raiders, you heah?"

"You are paying me enough to obey your orders. So long as I am in your employ, that is."

"Nothin' personal, Wilder."

"No offense taken." He took out a cheroot, touched a match to it, never losing his air of relaxed amusement. "Shall we have another touch of the bottle, please, sir?"

Jake grunted and poured. The man was more dangerous than a rattlesnake. The snake at least gave warning. Wilder had already made smirking faces at Claire, had patted Mrs. Bacon with pretended affection. The cowboys would be awed by his marksmanship and reputation. It would be necessary to keep the shotgun handy at all times.

"Still, that's the reason I hired the cross-grained bastid," he told himself. "If it comes down to Buchanan and us, we'll damn well need him."

He was not happy. He drank more than usual and had to be put to bed by Claire and Mrs. Bacon.

Peter Wolf had been listening and watching all day. Now it was dusk and he rode, knowing the circumstances, aware that the stolen Cross Bar cattle could be in only one place. They would not worry about him at the Casey ranch; he often went on scouting expeditions, sometimes to check the herdsmen, sometimes merely because he loved the land, knew the land, was part of the land.

His heart was heavy. It was the way Susan looked at Buchanan, the way she listened and followed his thoughts. Peter Wolf needed no more than that and the sisterly manner that she had long since adopted toward him to know his cause was hopeless. It had been so even before Buchanan; now it was dead.

He resolutely turned his mind toward Walking Elk and the young braves. They were headed on a downhill grade. They might despise him, but there was a slim chance that they might listen if he could find the right words. When he came close to the hidden arroyo he dismounted and proceeded afoot.

He heard the small clash of horns first, then a chorus of human voices. He crawled to a bush above the little clearing. They had made a clever Indian fire that ate its own smoke and gave a weird reflected light to the scene. They were actually dancing around the fire.

He lay on his belly. They were performing a ritual, one of the old ones that he could not identify. Walking Elk, always the leader, was a beat ahead of the others, leading them. It was not, Peter Wolf thought, a war dance. Neither was it a prayer. He thought from the jerky gestures that it was a mystic expression of spirit.

As he watched it seemed to him that Crazy Bird and the others were going through the motions, that only Walking Elk was in ecstasy, believing. Only Walking Elk crooned the old solemn tune with its insistent beat. Only his strong leadership kept them going through the motions.

Peter Wolf lay quite still for a long time. Occasionally he moved his limbs to keep the blood circulating. He wondered why he did not respond to the ceremony, the mesmerism of what was going on below. Walking Elk had been right—his white blood was predominant. The old ways meant absolutely nothing to him.

He thought instead of Susan, probably playing the piano for Buchanan and the others, mainly Buchanan. There had been no mistaking the flashes of her eyes when they harmonized on a tune familiar to both. He had to face it—if there had been a chance for him before, it was now departed.

So he was quite alone. Neither the red blood nor the white

could be fulfilled. The knowledge deepened in him, and for a moment he thought he would slide away and let events take their course.

He knew he could not. There was Mr. Casey and Mrs. Casey and the sheep and the knowledge that Jake Robertson was wrong. Even the girl Claire, with her openness, her declared wish for peace, deserved consideration. He could not care for her as he did for Susan, but he could admire her spirit. There was a quality called loyalty in which he strongly believed.

Down below Crazy Bird suddenly deserted the dancing circle and threw himself on the ground. Walking Elk spoke angrily to him. The other dancers slackened the pace. Walking Elk turned upon them and urged them to continue.

Crazy Bird crawled beyond the limited ring of light. Peter Wolf waited. The dancing continued. It was time to make a move. He snaked his way down to the floor of the arroyo. He moved inch by inch on his belly. He held his breath for a long moment, straining his eyes.

Crazy Bird was a dozen yards from the circle. Peter Wolf crept toward him. The Crow brave's ears picked up the faint rustle of movement and he tensed.

Peter Wolf put out a hand and whispered, "Quiet. It is I, a friend."

Crazy Bird opened his mouth, shut it again. He looked at the dancers, then began a silent crawl away from the fire. At a comparatively safe distance he stopped.

"Peter Wolf? What are you doing here?"

"Trying to save you."

"Are the whites coming here? To this place?"

"Unless you leave at once."

"Walking Elk says we shall steal more cattle. Drive them north. Sell them. Buy guns," Crazy Bird said.

"You believe that is possible?"

"They are killing one another. The man Buchanan killed one, crippled one."

"Then why not stay to fight with Buchanan against the cattlemen?"

"Walking Elk will not fight for the white eyes."

Peter Wolf asked, "You think this is wise?"

"When we were younger I was the crazy one. I was always in trouble. Walking Elk spoke much to the older ones. Now . . ."

"Now Walking Elk is possessed."

"It is you who said that."

"He believes."

"Yes. He believes. The others follow."

"And you?"

"He is my blood brother."

It was a sacred bond that could not be broken, Peter Wolf knew. Yet he felt that Crazy Bird was desperately unhappy, that he foresaw doom.

"Have you tried talking to him?"

"No. It is a dream. One cannot interfere with a dream."

This also was a truth. The Crow were a mystical people. It was impossible to deter them from a path on which their aspirations and beliefs had set them.

Peter Wolf said, "I know what you say. I know what Walking Elk wants. I understand it. But did you know that the cattleman has even now brought in six men to take the place of the two who were lost?"

Crazy Bird said, "I did not know."

"You know that is the way of the whites. They come in droves, like the cattle. They are too many."

"Is that why you stay with them?"

"I stay with the Casey family because they are good people. They make no war. They want only to live in peace."

"On the land of our forefathers. With their sheep."

"True. We know the land is ours. We also know we could not hold it against the whites. They are too many. They have too many guns. Crazy Bird, you know this is true."

"Sometimes you talk like a white man. Other times you talk like a Crow."

Peter Wolf said sadly, "How else would I talk?"

The dancers were faltering. One dropped, exhausted. Still Walking Elk pranced and chanted.

Crazy Bird said, "I believe you speak the truth. If there was anything that could be done . . . But there is not. You see him, how he is?"

Peter Wolf stared. He, too, had a goal, but he knew it was impossible to attain. Only an Indian with dreams could go on in the face of certain disaster.

He said, "There will be war between the cattlemen and the sheep people. I will be in it. Our side will have no more success than yours. So be it."

"The gods will decide," said Crazy Bird.

"Think. It is better to live."

"Yes. There is a maiden on the reservation who would pray with you."

Peter Wolf said, "May you live to wed her."

He rolled away. He wiggled past the brush that had concealed his approach. He had more trouble getting up the hill than descending. He crawled to his horse and led it safely away from the arroyo. Then he mounted and rode, his mind heavy with foreknowledge of what must take place.

SEVEN

THE CEREMONY WAS BRIEF, SINCERE, QUIET. Buchanan stood bareheaded with the three Caseys and Bascomb. The entire town had turned out for the burial of Arizona Jim Wetherby. Only Peter Wolf was absent. Since the town lacked a church, it was Coco who read a psalm from his tattered Bible and prayed in his earnest way for the departed soul.

As the people drifted away, Dr. Abrams and Bascomb approached, doffing their hats, solemn of visage. The doctor said, "Not in the nature of a wake, you understand, but Bascomb would open his place for a meeting of the minds. If you please."

Shawn Casey said, "I don't quite understand."

"Not open for customers," said Bascomb. "Want to talk with you all."

Susan said, "Come, Father, why not?"

They walked toward the saloon. A ranch wagon came down the street at a slow pace. Fritz Wilder and his men rode beside it. Dave Dare was the driver. Buchanan, towering above the crowd, could see into the body of the vehicle.

Semple lay on a rack of straw and blanket, his stump bound to his torso. Alongside him a blanket covered a still form.

Wilder rode to where Buchanan watched. "We're burying Jake's man on the Cross Bar, Buchanan."

"Uh-huh," said Buchanan.

"Nice job you and Arizona did. Of course, McGee and Semple were not top guns."

Semple said weakly, "You mealymouth bastid."

"Nor very smart," added Wilder. "I expect I'll be seeing you around, Buchanan."

"Uh-huh," said Buchanan. "Look sharp."

"I will. And I'll be quick."

"Uh-huh."

The wagon creaked on. Wilder touched his hat brim and showed white, even teeth. He wore gray trousers, a short black coat, a white hat with a black band. There was a glittering stone on his left hand. He rode with easy grace, straight-backed.

Susan said, "That man gives me the shivers."

"He has a high opinion of himself," Buchanan said. "Always did. Killed a few people in his time."

"Take away his gun and what you got?" asked Coco.

"That we won't never know," said Buchanan.

In Bascomb's they sat around a deal table. Drinks were proffered and accepted. Dr. Abrams took the floor.

"Arizona was a decent man, a good man. The only other law we have is Sheriff Bromberg. He chooses not to make his presence known in Sheridan."

"Robertson owns him," said Bascomb.

"This is a quiet little town unless the Cross Bar men ride in," said Dr. Abrams. "The farmers trade here, so does

Cross Bar and so do you people. Keeps us going. But there is going to be trouble; anyone can see it.''

"I'm afraid you're right," said Shawn Casey.

"Not your doin'," said Bascomb. "Nevertheless."

"We must have local law," said Dr. Abrams. "Now we know there is no use asking Mr. Buchanan to take the job—temporarily, that is."

"Uh-huh," said Buchanan. "Who's mayor of the town?"

"Never had one," said Bascomb. "Me and Doc and a couple good folks, we sorta do what's to be done."

"It was peaceful before Cross Bar began its shenanigans," said Mr. Abrams. "We didn't need much law."

"But now we got to have somebody. Is there anyone you know, Buchanan?" asked Bascomb.

Buchanan shook his head. "Not right now. Comes a time, gents, when you have to do for yourselves."

"We haven't a soul in town who could act as marshal."

"Not what I mean. One man, what can he do? All of you, that's a horse of a different color."

"All of us?"

Shawn Casey interposed, "Buchanan is absolutely correct. United, you are a force. You are the people."

"Everybody in this country owns a gun," said Buchanan.

"Everybody don't know how or when to use it," Dr. Abrams pointed out.

"That's when you have a drill," said Shawn Casey. "You call a town meeting. You tell them the problem. You explain that until a lawman can be hired they must act judicially but firmly, in the interest of the whole."

Dr. Abrams said slowly, "I believe you two make sense. I see what you mean. Even a gunslinger wouldn't go against a whole town."

Coco said, "Just a show of folks, seems to me like. Even the bad ones don't shoot folks ain't carryin' a gun."

"Part right," Buchanan agreed. "Only I'd have some people on roofs or out of sight who are ready just in case."

"Unfortunately," said Casey, "that's the way it would have to be."

Bascomb looked at the doctor. "You think it might work?"

"I think these good people have given us two alternatives. We knuckle under or we show we are not afraid."

"I'm somewhat afraid," said Bascomb. "Just my skin, that's all."

"Trouble usually starts in the saloon," Buchanan agreed. "You'd best rig up an alarm of some kind. Let people know when the goin' gets rough."

"That's a good idea," said Dr. Abrams. "A bell. A loud bell. People react to bells. As in case of fire."

"Yeah," said Bascomb, brightening. "Run it through the wall back o' the bar." He sobered. "Course, they might shoot me first."

Buchanan said, "Get yourself a greener. No man can face a sawed-off shotgun if he knows the man that holds it means business."

Bascomb gulped. "Yep. I've seen what it can do. Well, reckon we got no choice."

"We'll call a town meeting," said Dr. Abrams briskly. "And thank you people for your advice. I should have thought of it myself."

"You're a man who saves lives. Think of it along those lines," said Buchanan.

He arose and the others followed him outdoors. It was a beautiful day, too nice a day for Arizona to miss, he thought. He responded to greetings from the people on the street. They were simple folk, immigrants to the western country, some of long standing. Not violent themselves, but they were accustomed to tales of violence. How they would react without their lawman was something that would have to be seen. Buchanan had given them the best he could under the circumstances.

The Caseys had come in a carriage. He bade them good afternoon, mounted Nightshade and rode out onto the plain. He expected no attempt upon the sheep today on account of the funeral arrangements made by Jake. It seemed strange that there should be a graveyard inaugurated on Cross Bar—perhaps it had to do with Jake's devotion to whiskey.

Jake had always been a heavy drinker, but on occasion so had about every man Buchanan had known—including himself. Drunkenness had been responsible for so many of the gunfights he had seen that he often thoroughly agreed with Coco that whiskey was the curse of the West.

Arizona had not died because of booze. He had died defending Buchanan and the law, his concept of friendship, loyalty and duty. Semple had been crippled and McGee killed because of their sense of pride—and because of a distorted sense of their responsibility as hired guns.

Nothing was simple. There was Claire and Susan and Peter Wolf. There was Walking Elk and his wild young followers. There were cattle and there were sheep. And there he was, defending the concept of justice—as he saw it—in a fight that any fool could see was hopeless because of the overwhelming odds.

He shook his head and rode for the northernmost sheep camp. His shoulder ached. He shifted in the saddle to relieve the pain, trying to enjoy the perfect day. He rode across grass cropped so close to the ground that a mouse could not conceal itself among the blades. He sighed. Sheep versus cattle, it would always be a problem. Yet here he was, in the middle again. He longed for the peace of Billy Button's ranch in New Mexico, for the happy voice of his namesake, little Tommy Button.

So musing, he came within sight of the herd. Even at a distance he knew something was wrong. A breeze brought the bleating of the sheep to his ear. Men, small figures, ran.

Dogs, tiny, ran faster. He clucked to Nightshade and the ever-willing black horse flew like the wind.

A shot sounded. Nightshade ran more swiftly still. Buchanan loosened his rifle in its boot.

The sheep milled and began circling under the urging of the clever border collies. The men were tangled in a knot. A grazing horse threw up its head and whinnied. Buchanan came down like the wind, made a running dismount. Peter Wolf was engaged in battle with a burly man almost twice his size. Two inept herdsmen were warily trying to stop the fight.

Buchanan said, "Now, then." He fired a warning shot from the rifle.

The two futile herders jumped back. Peter Wolf hit the big man with a strong left hand. The man hit Peter Wolf with a low-ranging right.

Buchanan stepped between them, poked the rifle at the stranger and said, "You don't have much sense, do you?"

The man jumped back. One eye was swelling. He was crazy with rage. He yelled, "He jumped me over a damn dog. A mangy, one-eyed lousy mutt."

Peter Wolf said, "He would have shot Sandy if I hadn't come along."

"Sandy?"

"Sandy's old. He ain't mangy. He lost an eye protecting the herd against a wolf." Peter Wolf shook himself, adjusting his shirttail. "This damn fool is new."

Buchanan looked at the herders. They were Mexicans. They shrugged, agreeing with Peter Wolf but not anxious to get into an argument.

The big man said, "I just come for grub. They said there was some kinda war comin' up. The damn dog like to have bit me."

"The dog was trying to be friendly. This man's no damn good," said Peter Wolf.

The man lunged. Buchanan poked him with the muzzle of the rifle. He asked, "You got a horse?"

"Certain', I got a horse."

"Catch him up and make tracks," said Buchanan.

"You goin' to take the word of a damn breed and a couple Mexes agin me?"

Buchanan said, "I could let Peter Wolf whip you. Or shoot you, for that matter."

The man blinked, swallowed, stared. In an entirely different voice he asked, "Hey, are you Buchanan?"

"Uh-huh."

"Oh, hell." He backed away. "I'm . . . no hard feelin's . . . I'm on my way."

They watched him catch up a swaybacked roan, saddle with fumbling hands, mount and ride off.

Buchanan pointed. "What's that?"

Peter Wolf bent and picked up a six-shooter. "That's his gun."

"He was aimin' at Sandy."

The dog came forward, head cocked, at the sound of its name. It was a black and white, and it limped a bit. Buchanan reached a hand and Sandy sniffed at it, then returned to the herders as if it had done its duty.

"You took the gun away?"

"I kicked it outa his hand," said Peter Wolf.

The Mexicans both spoke at once in their native tongue. Buchanan answered them in kind, "I see. It was very fine, what Peter Wolf did. Yes, very fine." He returned his attention to the young man, asking quizzically, "Didn't it occur to you that you're wearin' a gun?"

"I wanted to punish him. He kicked Sandy."

"You figured to punish that big jake with your hands? Better than with a gun?"

Peter Wolf said, "If I'd've drawn . . . I mighta killed him. You see?"

Buchanan said warmly, "Uh-huh, you did what come

natural. Come on, let's you and me ride and take a look at that south herd.''

He nodded to the Mexicans, who smiled and gesticulated, then waved. They were far from home, but they knew their job of tending sheep. The north herd, he thought, was not in immediate danger. There was that ravine too close to the graze of the south herd.

As they rode side by side Buchanan said, ''You been missin' some lately.''

''Yes. I saw Walking Elk.''

''He show signs of comin' to his senses?''

Peter Wolf lifted a shoulder. ''Far from it.'' He related what he had seen and what he had learned from Crazy Bird. He ended, ''There is a bad thing coming there.''

''Very bad,'' said Buchanan. ''The new gun, Fritz Wilder, is a very dangerous man. If you meet up with him, do not try to kick the gun out of his hand.''

''I am not a gunslinger.''

''No need to be. Just be watchful and quick. Real quick.''

''Like you.''

''I learned it when I was younger'n you, Peter Wolf. That's the only reason I'm alive today.''

''It was peaceful here before the Robertsons came. There was no gunplay.''

''It is gettin' kinda serious when young men like Walking Elk begin their dances, isn't it?'' Buchanan said.

''A lamb or a sheep now and then. Not much. They did not threaten us.''

''But now?''

Peter Wolf stared off at the horizon. ''Now I don't know. When the vision is on them . . . But you know all that.''

''The Crow were once friendly to me. Saved me and some others a few years ago when we were in a tight spot.''

''I have heard the tale.''

''Now we've got Walking Elk and his braves. Any chance of getting Crazy Bird away?''

"There would be a curse upon him. Because they're blood brothers," Peter Wolf told him.

"Uh-huh."

They came to the edge of the graze. The sheep were munching away; the dogs were lying low, watchful but at ease. Indian Joe waved to them. Gowdy came and shook his head, saying, "Saw the funeral goin' to Cross Bar. Soberin', ain't it?"

"Dangerous," said Buchanan. "Did you see Fritz Wilder?"

"That's who it was, eh? The good Lord help us all." The fat man was truly agitated. "Robertson hired Wilder? McGee and Semple, they were nothin' like Wilder."

Buchanan said, "I been thinkin'." He looked to Peter Wolf. "Could this bunch be moved north?"

"To the other herd? It would be hard to do."

Gowdy said, "You come over the high land. No graze. Sheep move slow as the mountains."

Buchanan indicated the ravine. "Still and all. Lose 'em one way or the other."

"You reckon they'll come again?"

"With Wilder in charge they'll come. And soon."

Gowdy asked Peter Wolf, "What do you think?"

There was a long pause. Then Peter Wolf said, "It's somethin' that should be done. I can see it. Maybe Robertson will be satisfied if we move 'em."

Buchanan shook his head. "Don't believe that. You ain't leavin' enough grass for cows. He's got the bug in his ear. Like the man said, he don't want everything . . . just what's next door to him."

"You think he'll want to get you, too? Because of McGee and Semple and all?"

"There was a day when we was friends. Sort of. He's different now. The liquor seems to have got to Jake. I don't know him anymore."

A ram strayed from the herd, a raunchy-looking beast.

One of the dogs went silently to chivvy him back. The ram lowered its head and ran, trying to butt the dog. In another minute it was blatting its head off, on its back, skinny legs pawing the air.

Gowdy said, "That dog's a McNab. Trained to fight if need be. Nobody'll get us in the night when he and his brother are around."

Buchanan said, "There's a saddle tramp in the neighborhood." He took the man's gun from his belt and handed it to Gowdy, who examined it with satisfaction.

Peter Wolf said, "You'll need cartridges." He emptied his belt.

Gowdy said, "God, nobody wants a fight less'n me. If it comes, though, I'll be ready. I won't like it, but Casey's been awful good to us. Me and Joe, we'll be there."

"Let's hope it don't go that far," said Buchanan.

They mounted and rode back toward the Casey house. The afternoon was waning; the sun threw colors across sky and land. There was no more beautiful country, Buchanan thought. He mused aloud, "Only man can ugly up land like this."

"So said the Crow in another day," replied Peter Wolf.

"You seem to know a little of both. Indian and whites, what they're like, how they act."

"I wasn't always with the Caseys. I rode the line a while. I was in the towns as a boy. The padres taught me some." He was silent, then he said vehemently, "Now I know maybe too much. I want too much. You're a lucky man, Buchanan."

Buchanan eased a sudden ache in his shoulder. "Uh-huh. I'm plumb lucky to be alive. But wantin' too much is better than not wantin' at all, now, ain't it?"

"No!"

"You're a youngster, Peter Wolf," said Buchanan gently. "Time goes by, you'll learn. Keep wantin'. Keep hopin'. Do what you think's right. Hell, I ain't one for givin' advice, which is worth what it costs . . . nothin'."

They rode on. Buchanan knew very well what was hurting the youth. Susan Casey simply did not feel that way about him. She saw him as a brother. It was extremely dubious that she would ever think of him in any other way.

As the veteran of many a romance, he understood the problem. He knew very well that nothing in the world could be done about it, not by him, not by anyone but the reluctant girl herself. Further, he had not been unaware of Susan's smiles, bestowed upon him when she played the piano, whenever they were together. It was, he thought, tit for tat. He felt no urge toward the lively, comely daughter of Shawn Casey.

A few hours later they were all in the Casey parlor and Susan was playing hymns in memory of Arizona. Buchanan was uncomfortably aware of Peter Wolf's steady gaze—and of Susan's smiles. He had never felt more helpless. He begged off early and retired to his room, where Coco again applied the salve of the Crow girl to his wound. It was not a happy time.

EIGHT

Jake Robertson stared out at the little hill upon which they had buried McGee. He could see Boots Semple standing at graveside practicing a left-hand draw. The Colt fell out of Semple's hand and his curses floated on the air, unheard. Claire came from the house. It was early morning. Jake had his first drink in his fist.

She was wearing her divided skirt and a man's shirt with the top button undone, and her jawline was pronounced. She said, "Our own graveyard and a man with one arm trying to learn all over again to be a killer. Not to mention a slimy creature in fine clothes staring at me all day long . . ."

Jake interrupted, "If that Wilder makes one move onto you, just lemme know."

"Yes, and you with that sawed-off shotgun and your bottle. And Mrs. Bacon being more impossible every day. I'm beginning to hate Cross Bar, Papa. I'm beginning to truly detest it."

"Now, gal, just take it easy. There's certain things got to be. I had to hire the best, and Wilder's it."

"You didn't have to hire anyone. Our men tried to kill Buchanan. You should have admitted it and made peace. They are moving the sheep north, away from Cross Bar. That should be enough. Fire Wilder, talk with the Caseys. Compromise. Then we can all sleep well."

He shook a fist at the sky. "Just like a woman! Damn me. Tellin' me to give in, be satisfied with what you got. Not me. Not never!"

Claire's boot heels clicked on the veranda steps; her tiny silver spurs tinkled. She stopped and cried, "You'll lose it all! You'll lose your life!"

She ran for the corral, tears streaming down her cheeks. She caught up her horse, saw that the left hind shoe was missing a nail. She saddled and led the little bay to the blacksmith shop. Cobber was running his bright chain through his huge hands.

She said sharply, "Put that down and pay attention to your work, Cobber. There's too much fear of Buchanan around here."

He glared. "Fear? Me! I'll scrag him with this . . ." He retreated before her rage. "Yes, ma'am."

She watched him drive home the nail. They were all mad, she thought. All of them were blood-crazed. It was horrifying. She climbed aboard the mare and rode out. Maybe she would meet Peter Wolf. Now that the sheep were moving north, perhaps he would speak kindly with her.

She knew better; still she rode. She came to the slope leading to the hilltop from which Buchanan had witnessed the theft of the Cross Bar cows. Peter Wolf was atop the crest, sitting the roan, immobile, erect, staring into the distance. He seemed to be oblivious to everything but the scene to the west and below him. She came alongside and he put out a hand to stop her, still gazing, his face set and sad. She followed the direction of his staring.

She could see it all plainly in the bright Wyoming distance. The Indians were again into the Cross Bar herd. Bowlegs, the rider nearest them, was daydreaming. By the time they had cut out a few long-legged yearlings, he was too late to do anything but scramble for his rifle and fire it wildly, missing them by a country mile.

Dave Dare was also too far from the scene. Walking Elk and his men were into the trees before any sort of pursuit could be arranged.

She said, "Oh, no. That was bad."

His eyes were bleak. "It was very bad."

"Now Papa and that awful Wilder man will go after them."

"Sooner or later." He was talking half to himself.

"I tried. I talked to Papa. To the Caseys. You know I tried to make peace."

"Yes, miss. You tried. Buchanan tried."

"If they catch the Indians . . ."

"We know what will happen."

"You moved the sheep. We've done all we could."

"Yes. All we could."

She cried, "Peter, let's, you and I, get away!"

"Away?" he was confused.

"I have money in Texas. We could start a small ranch. Anything to get out of this."

He swallowed and said, "Miss Robertson, I scarcely know what you're gettin' at. What I know is, my place is here. Whatever happens I got to stick here."

"Don't you see it's hopeless? Papa's got all those gunmen. He'll kill the Indians and then he'll come for the Caseys. He's insane about the graze. He drinks too much; he listens to that awful Mrs. Bacon. There's nothing more I can do."

"I'm sorry. I see how it is with you. Yes, I can see. You got more common sense than the rest of your crowd."

"If you'd only help me. Take me away." She was

flushed, frightened at her own temerity, but she stood her ground. "I could be ready in an hour. Before it all starts."

He said, "Miss Robertson, you better go home. There's not a thing I can do except stay with the Caseys."

She could go no further. She said, "I'm sorry you can't . . . help me."

"I'd plain like to," he said. "I mean, seein' the way you feel, you oughta get away."

"Yes. I should. I won't. As you say, we must stick with our own."

"That's right."

"I'll still try to help."

"I'm sure you will, miss. But me, I believe it's gone too far. The Crow . . . the sheep . . . Buchanan . . . it's too much. Your papa and his hired guns will be on the warpath."

"Perhaps I can keep them away from the Caseys."

"You try and do that." He touched his hat brim. Frowning, he rode back toward the Casey place.

She gazed after him. Her tears did not run this time. She had almost declared her love for him. Love? She wondered. Infatuation? Or was it her desperate need to get away from Cross Bar and everything that had been happening there since she had come home?

It did not matter. The West, they said, was hardest on dogs, cattle and women. She turned back to face the inevitable when the news of the latest depredation came to her father.

When she arrived Jake was pacing the veranda. "I tell you, they're out to steal everything we got. The dirty redskinned thieves, they're makin war, that's what they're doin'."

Dave Dare said, "They hide awful good. We never come close to where they're herdin' them yearlin's."

Claire pleaded, "Papa, it's just a few head. You have

thousands. Let it go. Set a better watch. Bowlegs was not paying attention. I saw him, Papa.''

Fritz Wilder lit a cheroot. ''You're correct, Jake.''

''I know I'm damn right. Trouble is, it'd take a damn Injun to find the devils.''

Wilder said, ''You didn't take note? One of my men is an Apache. Name of Ramirez.''

''Then he can track.''

''Anybody. Anyplace.''

''What're we waitin' for? Get the boys together.''

Claire said, ''No! It just means more killing.''

''Get in the house, gal,'' said Jake. ''This is men's work.''

Claire was lost in the scramble. Wilder winked at her, and she resisted an impulse to punch him. She went into the house and up to her room. She was in utter despair, yet she was dry-eyed; her chin was firm.

They rode out in force, leaving Dave Dare and Bowlegs and the other cowboys behind. Ramirez, a scar-faced, slit-eyed little man, led the way. They picked up the trail where Walking Elk and his braves had vanished in the forest. The progress became slow. Ramirez examined tree trunks; bushes; dried, broken sticks. He was very thorough.

Only one rode beside Wilder, a good-looking young man named Reck. He wore a purple shirt and checkered pants and ornamented boots with silver-dollar spurs.

He said, ''How come the Injun's name is Ramirez? Ain't that Mex?''

Wilder replied, ''Apaches mix with Mexicans. And shut up.''

''If we see 'em, we shoot 'em,'' said Reck. ''So what?''

''They have ears like animals. So—shut up.''

''Oh, sure, Fritz.'' The youth grinned and fell back.

The others were all of a pattern. On first glance they looked to be ordinary enough outdoor horsemen. Close attention showed them to be hard, with eyes that did not ever seem to blink. They were from several walks of life. They had names like Chalk and Sawmill and Brick. One was black and seemed to have no name except "Hey you."

The trees thinned out. Ramirez suddenly raised his hand for silence. The riders stopped, discipline strong in them. Ramirez made signs and disappeared into heavy brush.

Nobody spoke; nobody moved. Insects buzzed; small animals rustled underfoot; a fawn switched its tail among the firs.

Ramirez came back, toeing in, going directly to Wilder. "They in arroyo. They got watch. No can get high gun."

Wilder said, "Then what?"

"Go quiet. No horses."

"These men are no good afoot."

Ramirez shrugged. "You want cows? You want Crow?"

Wilder said, "How about the watch? Can you take him?"

"*Sí.* But maybe shootin'."

"Fifty pesos if you make it."

"*Sí,*" said Ramirez. "The arroyo—straight ahead." He was gone like a shadow.

Reck asked, "You think so?"

"I think we must be ready. We hear a shot, we ride in."

"Not knowin' who shot it . . .?" Reck nodded. He enjoyed the gamble. His pale eyes were wide-spaced, rather blank. Sometimes he giggled to himself. He was the second-fastest gun in the group.

Wilder said, "It'll be head-on if Ramirez misses."

"Head-on, ass-on, it's action." Reck drew his revolver and twirled the cylinders. He was grinning.

Time rolled slowly by. Wilder repressed the desire to light a cheroot.

The shot came. Then there was a second shot. "Ride," said Wilder.

They rode in. The way was narrow. Wilder and Reck

were in the van. The opening among the trees was sudden and broad. They could see running figures. They fired.

One Indian stumbled and fell. The others were gone like wisps on the wind. The invaders found themselves eerily alone. The fallen Crow writhed but made no sound. Wilder rode up to him and dismounted. The cows were making their sounds in the makeshift corral.

Reck said, "Damn, they're like ghosts."

"Ramirez didn't make it. Send somebody up to check."

"This one's alive." Reck fingered his gun. "Lemme?"

"No," said Wilder.

"Maybe you didn't notice, but Brick's down."

"I noticed."

The man called Brick had a hole in his forehead. He lay in a disordered heap not far from the Indian.

Reck said, "You goin' to torture the bastid, Fritz?"

"No."

"Then what?"

"Round up the cattle and drive them back to the place where we came into the woods."

"What about the Injun?"

"Put him on Brick's horse and bring him along."

Reck shrugged, put away his gun and did as he was told. Wilder lit a cheroot.

On the rim of the arroyo Ramirez lay dead. Two men carried him down. Wilder nodded. "That's two of ours. We have one of them. We'll get the rest later. They need a lesson."

He rode back along the trail Ramirez had found for them.

Crazy Bird and three braves crept in the grass. They came to a vantage point. One of their band had died from his wounds during the flight. They watched while the other was tossed aside and Ramirez carried down.

Crazy Bird said, "Walking Elk's dream is over."

"Yes."

"They have him. We must try to rescue him."

"Yes."

But there was no heart in them. The sudden attack had taken their spirit. Crazy Bird knew it; nevertheless, they followed at a distance. When they came to the place Wilder had selected, they crouched, watching. Among them they had one musket and an old revolver and two bows with arrows.

It all happened very swiftly. Two men with rifles were guarding the scene. They saw Wilder uncoil a rope and throw it over a tree limb. They saw a loop being arranged around the neck of Walking Elk. They saw him spit at Wilder, saw the blow to the face he received in turn.

Crazy Bird said, "Do you want to die with my brother?"

There was a silence.

He said, "There is no chance. We will die and he will die."

They shook their heads. "Walking Elk had the dream."

"It is not said that we should die unless we could save him."

They murmured assent. Tears were in their eyes, but they knew they had no chance.

Two men dragged Walking Elk beneath the limb of the tree. Wilder pulled the rope taut. They all joined then and hauled. Walking Elk was lifted from the ground choking, his arms and legs jerking, blood streaming from his wound. Crazy Bird had the only reliable gun. He knelt. He took aim. He fired. The bullet struck Walking Elk in the head. Crazy Bird and the other Crow braves ran to their horses. They were gone before the white men realized what had happened.

It was morning when Buchanan found the hanging figure of Walking Elk. He had been riding to cover the rear of the sheep traveling north. He rode up and held the body in his sore left arm while he cut the rope with the bowie he had taken to carrying these days. He laid the Indian youth on the ground, noted the bullet hole in his head. He cut trail until he learned how many men had taken part in the lynching. Then he rode into the forest and backtracked all that had taken place the previous day. He climbed to the rim of the arroyo and formed his own picture of what had happened there. The trail of the stolen cattle was broad enough for a tenderfoot to trace. He heard the whinny of a horse. It was an Indian pony roaming loose.

He cajoled the horse, caught it up and rode back to where Walking Elk reposed. He put the dead body on the pony and headed toward the Crow reservation.

Buchanan saw the Crow young men as they came at him from four directions. He sat Nightshade and awaited them. They rode in slowly, scrutinizing him. Then one came close.

"I am Crazy Bird. Walking Elk was my blood brother."

Buchanan said, "I bring him to you," speaking in Crow.

"It is a good thing you do."

"It was a shameful way for him to die."

Crazy Bird rode close to the corpse, looked at the head. "It was my bullet that killed him."

"Good," said Buchanan. "It was brave."

"Do you know the men who came after us?"

"I reckon I do."

Crazy Bird gulped. "There are too many. Walking Elk had the dream."

"Peter Wolf told me of it."

"I did not share the dream. But I am not free. I must go to the old ones and mourn. I must do penance."

"That is for you to decide."

"You know our ways."

"Uh-huh," said Buchanan. "I respect your ways."

"You are not one of us. You cannot understand."

"May well be," said Buchanan.

Crazy Bird intoned, "We have seen the end of the dream.

From now we will fight no more. We will return to the old ones and follow their ways."

"As you say."

"You have taken our land; you have come with the blue-coats and the cattlemen and we are destroyed."

"Go in peace," Buchanan said. There was no profit in arguing that he did not own an inch of land, that he sympathized with them, that he did understand their problem. He knew that there was no solution. They rode away leading the pony that bore the body of Walking Elk. Their shoulders were bowed; they were in mourning for more than the dead warrior.

Buchanan turned Nightshade around. The echo of far-off shots came on a breeze. Nightshade pricked up his ears and was in motion before Buchanan could touch the reins. The sound came from the north.

The volume increased as he rode. He loosened the rifle in the scabbard. There was no question but that the sheep were being raided. When he saw riders as dots on the horizon he withdrew the rifle.

They were already departing before he came within range. He fired uselessly, merely to let them know that reinforcements were available.

Gowdy and Indian Joe were entrenched behind the dead bodies of sheep. He came to them and they arose shakily. Gowdy said, "God, I thought you was more of 'em for a minute there."

The dogs were scurrying, rounding up the frightened, milling sheep. Neither Gowdy nor Indian Joe was injured.

Buchanan asked, "Who?"

"A dude jasper and some uglies," said Gowdy. "They rode off to town."

Buchanan said, "Fritz Wilder."

"That was him? I didn't get a close look. Too busy tryin' to fight 'em off."

"You get any of 'em?"

"Nope. They moved too quick and left too sudden. I ain't in practice," said Gowdy apologetically.

"Never mind," said Buchanan. The bile was rising in him. "I'll have a word with Jake."

"You want us here? With the herd?"

He thought a moment. "Best push 'em until tonight. Then come into the house."

"Seems right," said Gowdy soberly. "Wilder, he's sudden and meaner than a basketful of rattlers."

"Might's well bring in the dead sheep for food."

"We'll do that."

Buchanan waved to them, and a few hundred yards away he stopped beneath a tree. Mrs. Bower had made him a lunch of bread and meat. He sat under the tree and ate it, calming himself as best he could, realizing that he could not charge in several directions at once.

When he had eaten, he remounted and rode to Cross Bar. He tied up Nightshade and walked to the veranda. Jake was in his usual spot, bottle beside him, shotgun at hand.

Buchanan said, "Jake."

"Buchanan. Have a touch?"

"No, thanks. Wanted to talk."

"No damn use. They stole my cows."

"You got 'em back."

"They killed two more of my men." Jake glared. Again his voice was hoarse and uneven. His nose glowed red.

"Not your workin' men. Your guns."

"I got guns to protect me."

"So they hang a young Indian."

"The Injuns stole my cows and killed my men."

"Your men attacked them. Two lives for a lousy twelve cows, Jake. Think on that."

"I don't got to think. I got to keep what I got and I got to expand. Expand. You understand that?"

"Uh-huh. It's called piggishness," said Buchanan.

"Your new man Fritz Wilder just shot a dozen sheep. No reason, just cut down on 'em."

"The hell with the sheep. Fritz got me back my cows and taught the damn redskins a lesson. That's the way she lays."

Claire appeared in the doorway. "Shame," she cried. "For nothing at all the blood is running. More graves on your hill. Is that what you're building, Papa, a graveyard?"

"You git back in the house, girl. This here is man talk."

"Men are certainly doing noble deeds hereabouts," she said. "Brave men shooting sheep."

"And young Indians," Buchanan added. "It's got to stop, Jake. I'm tellin' you true."

From Buchanan's right Boots Semple's voice came. "You ain't gonna live to tell nobody. . . ."

Buchanan spun and drew. Semple fired left-handed, and the bullet knocked Buchanan's hat from his head.

Buchanan shot him at the belt buckle. Semple folded slowly like a half-empty grain sack.

Claire cried, "Buchanan!"

Before he could turn a chain was around his neck. He gagged, floundering. Cobber yanked on his glittering chain.

Claire grabbed for her father's shotgun.

Buchanan choked, "No, girl . . . no!"

Cobber growled in his glee. He threw his weight into his effort. Buchanan went with the pull. They staggered backward. Buchanan could not breathe. He dug an elbow into Cobber's middle. He met muscle like pig iron. Still they went backward.

The world was beginning to turn black. He had never felt closer to death. It was excruciating, fighting for air. He had forgotten he had the Colt in his hand. He pointed it to the ground behind him. With his last remnant of strength he pulled the trigger.

Cobber howled with pain. His grip on the chain diminished. The bullet had clipped his foot. Buchanan fired again. Cobber fell away, sobbing. Buchanan reeled, coughing, seeking to fill his lungs. Claire still held the shotgun, pale, eyes like saucers. He motioned to her that all was over, turned to see Cobber on the ground, his right leg shattered.

He managed to walk to where Semple lay. This time the job was done. Semple lay in a pool of blood. He was dead. Buchanan looked at Jake, fixed in his chair, his mouth hanging open. "Now you've seen part of it. Next time, Jake, it could be you. Let Fritz Wilder advise you . . ."—he coughed through his pain—"and it'll happen."

Cobber was moaning. Buchanan went to him and looked down. "Maybe Jake'll have Wilder shoot you like they shoot horses."

Claire called, "Please, Mr. Buchanan."

He retrieved his hat, looked ruefully at the hole through the crown. "I do thank you for your try, Miss Claire. Trouble was, if you fired off that scattergun, you might've killed both Cobber and me. Ask your Papa."

He was weak as he walked to Nightshade, but he managed to keep his head high and his shoulders square. There was an angry red mark around his neck, and his left shoulder had begun to ache again. He still had a bit of difficulty in getting a full breath of air into his lungs. He mounted and rode out, not looking back to where Dave Dare was going to Cobber and Jake still sat in his chair for once without words. It had not, he thought, been a profitable visit. Jake's drinking had brought him under the spell of Wilder, no question about that. There were too many dead; too much blood had been shed. There was, he knew, more to come.

When he arrived at the Casey stable it was late afternoon and his throat ached. Coco was tending the black lamb.

Buchanan said, "I hope he's okay. He got us into this." His voice was a raven's croak.

"Lemme look at you," said Coco. There was a scarlet ring around the thick neck. Coco said, "They try to hang you?"

"They hung Walking Elk," said Buchanan. In slow, hoarse, measured tones he related the events of the day.

Coco said sadly, "Guns and rope and chains. We got ourselfs into the biggest mess yet, didn't we?"

Buchanan nodded.

"You figure there's any way outa this?"

Buchanan shook his head.

"You reckon Cross Bar's comin' for us?"

"Wilder," Buchanan whispered.

"The man's a devil."

Buchanan nodded again.

"No help from the Crow?"

Buchanan again shook his head.

Coco petted the lamb. Johnnybear was removing the saddle and bridle from Nightshade, pouring oats into the bin, silent as always. Buchanan started for the house.

Bascomb rode into the yard on a heaving hired hack. He called, "Buchanan! Wilder and them shot up the town."

Buchanan turned wearily and asked in his weak voice, "Anybody hurt?"

"Two, three. Doc and his wife are takin' care of them. They sent me out here."

Buchanan said, "You weren't ready."

"It ain't easy." Bascomb flushed. "I ain't no fighter. Sheridan people ain't ready for this kinda doin'. Figured if they got those gunslingers mad enough, they'd burn the town down."

"Not the way to figure." He choked, began again. "On the roofs. If you don't fight 'em, they'll come again. And again. Those are bad men, Bascomb."

"If we talked to Jake Robertson?"

"I've done that."

"Nothin'?"

"Less." He didn't want to tell what had happened. He only wished to be alone, to rest his throat, to try the miraculous Crow herb cure, to think things out. He had killed another man and he did not ever want to kill.

He asked, "They need me in town?"

"Well . . . Doc thought maybe . . . I dunno."

Buchanan said, "I'll be there."

Bascomb brightened. "I'll tell 'em." He turned the nag around with some difficulty and was gone.

Coco said, "You got no right goin' anywhere."

"Let me get some food. Johnnybear, wipe down Nightshade; he can go again." It hurt a lot to talk, but talk he must.

"I'm goin' with you," said Coco.

"Appreciate it." Buchanan went into the house. He did not remember a day in which so much had occurred. He was worn out with it. For a time he wished he had never seen the little black lamb. Then he was with the Caseys, and he realized that he did not wish any such thing.

Fritz Wilder said, "You let Buchanan come here, kill Semple and cripple your blacksmith?" He laughed. "Can't I leave you alone for a minute?"

Jake said, "They jumped him. I warned 'em. I told 'em not to try Buchanan."

"Scared. He has you all frightened to death."

"Not by damn! Careful. You move careful around that fella. Knowed him for years. Careful." Jake was quite drunk.

Wilder said, "Truly, you must know you're wrong. A man like Buchanan can only be taken by force. Coupled with brains. Surprise is the element. You know you have to get him."

"Gettin' him ain't goin' to be that easy. Nohow." Jake drank.

Wilder said, "He's even got the sheepherders fighting. They fired on us today. One came close to hitting me. We could have charged them, but it would have been dangerous. Sooner or later we must get them."

"Damn sheep."

"I wouldn't be surprised if Buchanan set the Indians on you. He's friendly with them; everyone knows that."

"Goddam Injuns."

"If we got rid of Buchanan it would put a stop to everything."

"Damn Buchanan shoulda stayed in New Mexico."

Claire came onto the veranda. "Papa, don't listen to him."

"You stay outa this, gal."

"It was bad enough with McGee and Semple. Now they're dead and Cobber may lose a leg and you want to keep up this war. I say it stops!"

"It ain't for you to say!"

"Are you going to listen to this . . . this killer . . . or to your daughter?" Her lips trembled.

"I say you git to your room and stay there," shouted Jake.

Her strong chin asserted itself. She said, "Don't you try that, Papa."

Fritz Wilder said, "Maybe Miss Claire is worried about the half-breed she's been seeing."

"The what? You mean that Wolf fella?" Jake rose from the chair, staggered, regained his balance.

Claire said, "What are you going to do, Papa? Shoot me with that shotgun of yours?"

"Handsome young man," said Wilder.

Jake choked, managed to wheeze, "Now, go to your room. And you damn well stay there till I tell you that you can come out. A damn breed! My daughter."

Wilder smiled sweetly. "It's probably nothing serious. Still, she's been seen with him."

"Git!" Jake was close to apoplexy. "To your room!"

Claire looked at him, then at Wilder. "So. That's it. It is this . . . this beast. All right, Papa. All right."

She bent her head and went into the house. She went up the stairs and into her room. She heard her father yelling at Mrs. Bacon to keep watch on her. She heard Wilder saying again and again that they must attack, that they must get the jump on Buchanan and the Caseys if necessary. The gunslinger was partly insane, she thought, and the liquor had warped her father beyond recognition.

She changed into her divided skirt and a woolen shirt. She donned her boots. She took a small-caliber Smith & Wesson from a drawer.

Outside her door she heard Mrs. Bacon wheezing. She called, "Come in, please."

Mrs. Bacon entered. Claire drew back the gun and hit her behind the ear. Mrs. Bacon hit the floor.

Claire walked down the back stairs without haste. She went to the stable. Dave Dare was currying a horse. She said sweetly, "Saddle up the pinto, please? I'm going for a ride." She did not want the black mare her papa had given her.

"Anything for you, Claire." He obeyed.

She said, "Don't tell Papa I've gone. He's in a snit."

"Whatever you say, Claire."

She mounted the horse without aid and rode out the back way. There were tears in her eyes and her heart was like lead. She headed straight for the Casey place.

Her mind raced as the pony galloped across the plain. She was amazed at her temerity; then she was not. Her first thought had been of Peter Wolf. They would kill him. Why should she care? He had not even understood her near declaration. His mind was far from her.

Then she thought of her parents. Her mother had been a gentle creature. Her papa had always been kind and loving when she was young, but he was often away, too busy extending his holdings to pay much attention to the home fires.

When her mother sent her away to school, he had become almost a stranger.

And when her mother died, he had taken to the bottle. Perhaps it was because he had loved her so. In view of the entrance of Mrs. Bacon so few months later, she doubted that. He was a tough man, as he declared. He thought in terms of possessions, of power that went with wealth. He was not much different from others she had met—but he was her father.

It was not that she was against wealth, comfort, belongings. And it was not entirely her love—infatuation?—for Peter Wolf. Some inner force was driving her, some sense of right and wrong.

She came to the Casey place with her mind clear. There were things to be said and done. She swung down from the pony and marched to the door of the house.

Susan Casey answered. She stared at Claire. "What do you want here?"

"I don't want anything except to talk," said Claire. Her hair was flowing, unbrushed. Her cheeks were pink, her eyes bright. "I came to warn you."

"We've had plenty of warnings," said Susan. However, she stepped aside so that Claire might enter.

"Buchanan will listen to me," Claire said. She saw the quick reaction of the girl. "He knows what can happen. Fritz Wilder is, I believe, crazy. He's talking Papa into attacking you to get to Buchanan."

"Coming here, you mean?"

"I tried to talk to Papa. He's . . ." She bit her lip. "He drinks too much. He won't listen. Wilder has him mesmerized or something."

Susan said, "You're scared, aren't you?"

"Not for myself."

"You come here and warn us? You?" Susan was incredulous. "Is this a trick?"

"What kind of trick? Am I asking you to do anything?

Am I trying to lead you into a trap? I'd like to talk with Buchanan, please.''

They had edged their way into the house. Susan said, "He's in town. Your . . . your father's men shot people last night."

"I know. That's one of the reasons I'm here. Can't you see?"

Susan said slowly, "I . . . I reckon I do see. You said it before. You want peace. I thought you were fakin'. On account of . . ." She broke off.

"On account of Peter Wolf. I see."

Susan squirmed. "I didn't mean to—"

"Peter doesn't want me."

Susan stared. "You . . . spoke to him?"

Claire took quick steps, her spurs jingling. She said, "What a nice room. So warm. You must be happy here."

"Why . . . sure."

"Your mother and father, they're sweet people."

"They're the best." Susan twisted her hands. "Your ma is dead. Your father drinks and . . . I see. I see." She reached out to stop Claire's pacing, taking her by the arm. "Come on into the kitchen. We'll have coffee. Buchanan will be back soon. I hope."

Claire said, "I'm afraid soon might not be quick enough. Wilder was talking hard to Papa. Bad talk, mean. They want Buchanan so much they'd kill anyone got in their way."

Susan said, "Coco is with Buchanan. Peter is watching. The others are in the barn. There are always guns around since it started. There's nothing more we can do right now." She slipped her arm about Claire. "Come."

Claire's hand went to her mouth. Up until this show of kindness and sympathy she had been under control. Now her lip trembled. She braced herself.

In the kitchen Mrs. Bower was feeding Johnnybear. She frowned, then smiled when the two girls came to the table.

135

Johnnybear's brown eyes were wide as, surveying the scene, he backed to the door.

Susan said in her direct manner, "Johnnybear, Mrs. Bower, Miss Robertson came here to warn us. There might be a fight. I'll go and tell father and mother about it."

She went out the rear door. Johnnybear stared at Claire. He bowed, swallowed and followed Susan. Mrs. Bower sat opposite Claire at the table.

"Your pa must've gone crazy. We don't mean any harm."

"My father is . . . is not himself." Claire choked on the words.

"The Caseys are the nicest folks in the world." Her violet eyes probed at Claire. "You want peace. You said so; I believe you."

"I thought if I came here . . . Now I don't know."

Mrs. Bower moved to a cabinet and took down a silver flask. She poured generously into Claire's coffee. "Brandy. You're pale as a ghost, girl."

"Thank you." Mrs. Bower was an oddly good-looking woman, she realized. She moved with grace. Her violet eyes had darkened.

"I wasn't always housekeeper to sheep people," the housekeeper was saying. "My husband and I had a spread once. In Texas."

"Texas? You know about cattle?"

"I knew your father," she said bluntly. "Oh, he didn't know us. When Charlie was killed and I lost the place, your father bought it. Took it, you might say."

"He stole it?"

"No. Just had the cash. You were in school too long, girl. You got good notions but you don't know how it is. You don't know how Buchanan is."

"I . . . I know he's a very brave man."

"Oh, yes. I'll bet you thought if you came here and Peter

Wolf saw that and Buchanan was here and all—you could stop the fight.''

"I . . . didn't think that far.'' She knew her color had been restored. Her cheeks were warm.

"Took me a while to get straight, y' know.'' Mrs. Bower drank coffee, keeping her eyes on Claire. "I got to know people. Men. Lots of men. Buchanans are scarce. Wilders are scarce too. Mostly, men are in between. A boy like Peter Wolf, he's rare. Not much chance for him exceptin' with innocents like the Caseys. The Caseys don't know prejudice.''

Claire was silent. This woman was wiser than she ever could be. She could feel it.

Mrs. Bower went on. "I knew Liz Bacon a bit, too. When your father picked her up she was runnin' a house in El Paso.''

"A . . . a house?''

"Oh, it was a high-class house. But she drank too much.''

"Yes. She drinks with Papa.''

"I'd bet on it. And agrees with every dumb thing he says or does. Right?''

"Right.''

"And now Fritz Wilder is callin' the turn,'' Mrs. Bower said.

"Yes. He's a madman.''

"Maybe. Meantime, he wants Buchanan. And why does he want Buchanan? Because he's a gunslinger, and if he kills Buchanan his name'll go up and down the country. If he does it fair and square people will kowtow to him. Whether they like it or not, they'll have a certain respect for him. It's the way of the country.''

"But that's terrible.''

"That's the way it is. School didn't teach you that. So now you can't come here and change things. Maybe your papa would want to call it off because you were here, but as soon as you left it would be on again. Nothin' can stop it when a man like Wilder comes after a man like Buchanan.''

"Papa only wanted to save the graze from the sheep. He's wrong about that. I thought it could be straightened out by talking, compromising. I tried."

"We know that. Even the Caseys don't realize how it can build and build. Buchanan picks up a little black sheep and all hell breaks loose. Well, it was crackin' before that. You bein' here won't change a thing."

"What should I do?" Claire asked. The woman's confidence, her straightforwardness, was commanding.

Mrs. Bower took the makings from her apron pocket and rolled a cigarette. She struck a match, inhaled, blew smoke. "Girl, I ain't one for buttin' in. But if I was you I'd take off right now. You either go to Cross Bar and try to talk some sense into your papa . . . or you go to town and pray a lot."

"I can't go home."

"Buchanan's in town tryin' to make brave men outa cowards. You might run across him on the way."

"I . . . don't know."

"Peter Wolf can't help you now." Again she felt herself blushing.

Mrs. Bower said, "I been around and I got eyes. Girl, he's in love with Susan."

Claire gasped, then quickly recovered. "I thought as much. Mrs. Bower, you're a wonder." She got to her feet. "I'll be heading for town."

"I'll make your manners to the Caseys." She smiled. "I reckon you'll be around at the showdown. One way or the other. Like I said, I know folks pretty good. You remind me of myself before I growed up."

"Thank you." She knew she was being paid a backhanded compliment. She was able to return the smile. She ran through the house. She could hear the voices of the Caseys in the backyard. She hesitated. Then she got into the saddle and rode for town.

Her mind cleared as she traveled the ten miles. Mrs. Bower had stunned her with the insight she had displayed. Claire had suspected that Peter Wolf was in love with Susan. She had not wanted to admit it fully, but all the signs had been there for her to see. She would cope with that later, she thought. Now was the time to use her intelligence.

She came into Sheridan before sundown. There were people in the streets, more than she had ever seen. She saw Dr. Abrams coming out of Bascomb's and pulled up.

He said, "Ah, Miss Robertson. I'm afraid you won't find a welcome here at this time."

"I know." She tied up and came close to him. "Doctor, I must see Buchanan at once. They'll be coming after him."

"They?"

"The gunmen my father hired." She stood straight and looked him in the eye. "I'm against them. I'm here to warn Buchanan. Believe me, please."

Dr. Abrams frowned. "Why, I do believe you, child. I remember Buchanan telling us about you. Come, you must stay with us."

"I have to see Buchanan."

"My dear," he said sadly, "Buchanan tried to bolster the men of this town for an hour. I doubt that he succeeded. Then he and Coco Bean rode out to warn the herders, your father's herders."

"I missed him." Her spirits fell again. She said dully, "If you'll be so kind. I'd be glad to have shelter. I guess I need it."

People stared at her as she led the pinto down the street to the Abrams house. No one spoke, out of regard for the doctor, but she could feel the animosity in the air. One way or another war had come to the country, and her father had brought it. She must, she realized, do a lot of growing up in the next hours and days.

NINE

Coco said, "You sure told 'em what the Lord told John. But did they listen?"

"With their ears they listened," said Buchanan. They were riding side by side to check the position of the sheep herds.

"That's just about it," Coco nodded. "Must say I can see how they feel. They ain't used to gunplay. They're citizens."

"They had a lesson from Wilder. You'd think they'd learn."

"People just don't learn that easy," said Coco.

"Looks like the herders got together," said Buchanan.

They had come within view of the sheep. The dogs were busy running around the perimeter. The Mexican herders were looking out. Gowdy and Indian Joe came toward Buchanan and Coco on horseback. Following them were the fighting dogs and one-eyed Sandy.

Gowdy said, "Lookin' for you to show. Indian Joe did a little scoutin'. They're formin' up at Cross Bar."

Indian Joe nodded. "Like a blue-shirt troop."

"You're real sure?" Buchanan's alarm was patent. "They start out yet?"

"They're about to."

"No doubt about it," said Gowdy. "They're comin' for you and for the Caseys. Mebbe they ain't sayin' they're after the Caseys, but it'll come to that."

Buchanan said, "We'll ride ahead. Come in as fast as you can."

"We'll be there."

It was darkening. The ground flew beneath Nightshade's feet. Coco followed several lengths behind. Buchanan felt stark alone with his thoughts.

He had grown fond of the gentle Caseys and their feisty daughter. Coco had been right about the town; the timid folks had listened to him, agreed with him—but they would never take action. He felt the heavy load on his shoulders as he seldom had before.

The hanging of Walking Elk stuck in his craw. A man who would order such a deed would stop at nothing. Wilder was beyond belief, a cold monster capable of rape, pillage, all the violence known to mankind.

He had known horse thieves, rustlers, gunmen, pimps, card sharps, and the rest of the riffraff of the shifting western frontier. They had come in all sizes and sorts. Few of them were, he thought, basically evil. Jake Robertson, a Texan, a rancher, a family man of sorts, had hired this creature and was backing him. It seemed incredible—and yet it was true and he must accept the fact.

Jake probably did not mean physical harm to the Caseys. But once the fight started, this signified nothing. Dave Dare and the cowboys would be caught up in the action; they had their own grudge against Buchanan. Once begun, it would be total war.

He tried to make plans. The odds were too great. He could not send the women away in the night. Little Johnnybear might make it, but where would he go?

He thought fleetingly of the girl, Claire Robertson. She might well be the sole survivor.

Peter Wolf would come in. With Gowdy and Indian Joe that was three to add to himself, Coco, Casey and the females. Mrs. Bower might be a help; she had a certain air about her that he had discerned. Susan would give her all; she was that kind of a person.

It was far from enough.

He dismounted in the yard, haste riding his back. The stable had been built far enough away to prevent a fire from spreading to the stone house. He loosened the girth of his saddle, tied the bit to the horn. He ran into the barn and found Johnnybear at his chores.

He said, "Son, they're comin' at us. Get the horses out. Turn 'em loose." He found Nightshade's halter. "Same with the corral. Throw water on the straw and hay. Don't be too long about that. When you hear 'em, you take off. You understand?"

Johnnybear nodded, imperturbable. "I've thought they would come."

"Just do as I say. Maybe you can make the reservation."

Johnnybear did not repond. He was already obeying orders. Buchanan ran outside and fastened the halter on the big black horse. He unlimbered his saddlebags and took the rifle from the boot. He said, "You're on your own. Get goin'."

He patted the rump of the knowing horse, and Nightshade trotted off into the darkness, not for the first time on his own.

Buchanan shouldered the bags, looked around. A lantern gave a feeble light. The black sheep made a sound. He said, "What the hell, you started it all." He picked it up and carried it into the kitchen.

Mrs. Bower looked at him and nodded. "They're comin'."

"Uh-huh."

She handed him a glass of milk. "You'll need food. I'll rustle up somethin'."

He put the sheep on the floor. It skittered on skinny legs. "It won't be in the way."

"No," she said. "We won't let anything get in the way."

"Is there plenty of ammunition?"

"I saw to that long ago." She opened a closet. In it were rifles and boxes of shells. "A blind man could see this comin', Buchanan. The Caseys just don't know about the way things are."

"Uh-huh. Two herders and Coco. They'll need grub."

"The Caseys had supper. I'll throw somethin' on the stove."

The sound of the piano came from the parlor. Buchanan shook his head. "Won't be time for that."

"It don't hurt anything."

He said, "You're mighty cool and calm, missus. You're quite a woman."

"Thought you might notice." She had white, even teeth, and there were slight lines at the corners of her eyes. "I seen the elephant, Buchanan."

He nodded toward the closet, "I'll bet six, two and even you can shoot one of them."

"You win." She was moving with swift grace putting food together. "I don't see how we can win this one, though."

"Twixt you and me and the barn door, I don't neither," he said. "Howsome-ever . . ."

"You should have cut out. Glad you didn't, though."

"You see the gal?"

"What gal?"

"That Claire Robertson. She came to warn us. I sent her to town hopin' she could catch up with you."

"Missed her. Just as well she's out of it," Buchanan said.

"She'll never be out of it. She's got a conscience, that one." There was admiration in Beth Bower's voice. "I put her onto Liz Bacon. Just in case."

"You know about the Bacon woman?"

"Plenty. Figured you knew."

"None of our business in a way. I mean, Jake's gone to the hogs altogether, seems like."

She produced a flask, winking at him. "A bit of the dog-hair that bit Jake?"

"Uh-huh."

She poured into jelly glasses. They sat a moment in silence. He hated to go to the Caseys with the news. Susan was playing "Camptown Races," bright and gay. The Caseys were singing.

The woman said softly, "Life gets all mixed up."

"Uh-huh."

"The Robertson gal and Peter Wolf."

"Uh-huh."

"Susan and guess who?" She cocked her head to the side.

"I think I hear Coco comin' in," he said hastily.

"I wouldn't open my big mouth if it didn't look like it might be curtains," she said. "You know it anyway. Just keep it in your head, Buchanan. Kindness helps."

It was Coco in the yard, and the herdsmen were close behind. Buchanan looked at them through the window. "Kindness. Uh-huh."

Mrs. Bower went to the closet, took down a rifle and began to load it with expert hands. "Peter Wolf, Claire Robertson. Susan Casey. And you."

"Woman, I haven't got time to palaver with you." He smiled at her.

"You could do worse." She returned the smile and continued loading rifles.

He called out the back door. "Gowdy, you and Indian Joe on the roof. Get shells from Mrs. Bower here. Coco, you turn all the stock loose, then come into the house."

Coco said, "They're ridin'. We seen 'em."

"Get movin', all of you."

Buchanan went into the parlor. The music had stopped at the sound of his voice. The Caseys were standing, calm, composed. Shawn asked, "Is this the way it must be?"

"We tried everything else," said Buchanan.

"The girl?" asked Susan.

"Missed her. She's in town."

"Lucky girl," said Susan. "What about Peter?"

"He's out there. Maybe that's good."

"No help from town?" asked Shawn.

"Afraid not," Buchanan said.

"What should we do?"

It always came down to that. He had to take charge. He said, "Heavy furniture against the doors. It's a stone house, which is mighty fine. I'm puttin' men on the roof."

Mrs. Casey said, "We haven't a chance against so many."

"There's always a chance," said her husband.

She took his hand. Susan went to them and they embraced. Buchanan went to the window and looked out. There were stars and the promise of a three-quarter moon. Under Wyoming sky that was enough light. He said, "Turn down the lamps. If there's shootin', be ready to douse 'em."

Mrs. Bower came from the kitchen bearing rifles. She began to place them near the windows. She said, "Coco and Johnnybear are missin'."

"I told Johnnybear to get away." He paused. "Coco, he hates guns. He won't shoot anyone. He wouldn't be any good in here."

"He might be . . ."

Buchanan said, "Coco's my best friend in the world. He'll do his best wherever he plans to do it." Buchanan put his concern for his friend away in the back of his head. It was necessary to think of the immediate present.

He wore both revolvers. The bowie was strung behind his neck. The derringer was in his belt buckle, where it always reposed. For a man of peace he was overloaded with weapons.

Two men on the roof, two inside the house, two out in the dark—that was it against the force to come. Three women, good women, he thought, who would not go into a tizzy. He had to add them to the defense. He would rather they were not present, but as long as they were he must accept the fact. It occurred to him that he could not die in better company.

Johnnybear was riding bareback on a sorrel pony he had been allowed to break for himself. In his head was the knowledge of the Crow Indian, his heritage, the great myth. In his heart was love of the white people who had been so kind to him, who had nurtured him, made him one of their own; and in his soul was a prayer that he might succeed in his mission.

Peter Wolf was on the plain, keeping well out of sight, trailing the crew from Cross Bar. In his heart was love for Susan Casey. He knew that the situation was desperate, but in his soul was devout dedication to honor, the honor of both red man and white.

Waiting in secure hiding behind a growth of brush outside the perimeter of the impending fight was Coco. His love for Buchanan was in his heart. In his soul was a longing for peaceful days when the guns would stop shooting.

In the town Claire Robertson pleaded with Dr. Abrams and Bascomb to help. Her throat was sore from talking. In her heart was her hopeless love for Peter Wolf. In her soul she wept for her errant father.

* * *

Buchanan could see them well enough. The cavalcade remained beyond rifle range, spread out, revealing a buckboard in the center. Mrs. Bacon held the reins. Jake swayed on the hard seat.

Buchanan said, "This is pure bad. Jake's too drunk to ride. His brain's scrambled like a pan of eggs."

"Putting Wilder in charge," said Shawn Casey. "Sad."

The buckboard lurched forward, the horsemen deployed. When his voice would carry, Jake steadied himself and the woman reined in.

"Tom Buchanan!"

Buchanan opened the door. Susan gasped, "No," but he shrugged and stepped outside.

"Jake, go home. Forget this business. Sober up."

"You done crossed the line, Buchanan. I . . . I got the last word for you. Git out. Git on your hoss and make tracks. Gimme your promise you won't come back. 'At's all I want."

"Go home and think about that. You're tellin' me to turn tail and run? You're real, complete loco, Jake."

"You got women in there. You want them to get hurt?"

"You want me to run and leave 'em?"

"It's on your head, Buchanan. You done me dirt."

"You did yourself dirt when you hired Wilder. Tell him I said so," Buchanan replied. "Now hear me, Jake. I could shoot you to pieces where you sit."

The woman's hands jerked at the reins, the team balked and neighed.

Buchanan went on, "I prob'ly should do just that. It ain't my way, and you know it or you wouldn't dare to come so close. Best you get on with your business. Best you go home, Jake. I'm tellin' you for the last time."

The wagon almost tipped over. Jake cursed and seized the reins. The buckboard spun crazily around and the horses broke into a run. The conference was over.

Buchanan closed the door and faced the Caseys. "It

wouldn't help a smidgen if I went out there and got killed. Wilder would have a gun posted to cut me down. All I can do is stick and fight. You see that?''

''We see it,'' said Shawn Casey.

''I got to tell you. They'll shoot out the windows. Lucky the house is stone. They'll hit the barn, but the stock is gone from there. Keep your heads down exceptin' when I say to fire. Don't waste bullets. We got water and grub, and Peter Wolf's out there and he ain't about to run. Give Coco a chance and he'll do his part. You got to get used to bullets flyin' around you. Wilder, he don't care if he kills a woman or a child. Wilder is loco.''

''We understand,'' said Susan. She was pale, but there was a light in her eyes. ''Where do you want us?''

''Mrs. Bower in the kitchen. The rest of you pick a wall. If they charge, shoot low. Man or horse, it's better'n a wild shot.''

Mrs. Casey murmured, ''That I should live to see the day! I could never shoot even a bird.''

''Men are more dangerous,'' Buchanan said. ''And more deservin'.''

He watched from behind the bulwark of the Caseys' fine dining table. Wilder was giving orders; he sensed that. The men were scattering. He dimly recognized Dave Dare and the other cowboys. Wilder remained at center stage with Reck, Chalk, Sawmill and the ones he didn't know. It was not a big force, but it was capable of heavy gunfire. There would be no brave charge. They would sharpshoot and maintain a seige. They hoped to flush him out into the open. Afterward they felt they could scare the Caseys from the country.

He held the rifle ready. The first shot came, shattering glass. Now the fight was joined; now he could shoot without compunction.

He said quietly, ''Keep your heads down low. Don't try to find a target. Main thing is to keep steady.''

There were indeed no targets. Wilder was smart, no doubt about that. It would be an Indian fight, he thought. They'd circle and keep low and start fires. They'd stay out of the light of the fires and shoot away, counting on inevitable panic.

Mrs. Bower called from the kitchen, "The dogs. What about the dogs?"

"Can you see them?"

"Yes. They're in the yard, prowlin' around."

"Bring 'em in," said Buchanan.

The dogs came into the house. They made no sound. Mrs. Bower fed them and they remained in the kitchen. Buchanan looked in and saw that they seemed to be looking to old Sandy for leadership. The maimed dog lay on his side, his one eye bright as if waiting for action.

"Women and dogs," said Buchanan to himself. "Hell of a way to fight a war."

He went back to his post. Now the shots came in rhythm, shattering glass, thumping into the sturdy table, crashing into the pictures on the wall.

"Steady," said Buchanan again.

They were steady. They were good people, strong in their silent way. Even Susan was well under control, fingering the rifle but hunched down, patient.

Now a riderless horse appeared in the near distance, running wild. Shots were fired, but it came on unharmed.

Susan exclaimed, "That's Peter's horse!"

"Keep your head down," said Buchanan sharply.

"Poor Peter," whispered Mrs. Casey.

Buchanan said, "Susan, open the door."

She moved quickly, unlocking the heavy portal. Buchanan crouched, staring. In a moment he was sure of his eyes. It was Coco and he was running doubled over. Buchanan stepped outside and began firing. He laid down a barrage into the shadows beyond his line of vision.

Coco staggered, caught himself, came on. Susan ran past

149

Buchanan. Casey and his wife were now firing into the distance beyond Coco as well.

It seemed hours before they knew what was taking place. Coco came closer, closer. Over his shoulder was Peter Wolf. Both were covered with blood.

Susan knelt and fired her rifle. Buchanan ran and took Peter Wolf from Coco's back. They all retreated into the house, stumbling, fighting for breath.

Shawn Casey closed the door behind them. His wife went to Peter Wolf. The wound was in his chest, high on the right. He was pale from loss of blood.

Coco said, "I was tryin' to get close. Too many. Scattered around too much. Peter, he come ridin' and shootin' like crazy. Wilder shot him."

"So you picked him up," Buchanan said.

"The horse got away. Peter don't weigh all that much," said Coco. "Couldn't leave him, now, could I?"

Peter Wolf said weakly, "He carried me half a mile, I swear. No man could do that. But he did it."

"Couldn't leave him." Coco's chest heaved, sweat ran from him. "They're settin' there, Jake and the woman and Wilder. They're cookin' up somethin', Tom."

"Uh-huh," said Buchanan. He thought he knew what they were plotting. They could not burn a stone house and barn. It would be explosives. It had to be dynamite or gunpowder, whichever was at hand.

Peter Wolf said, "Give me a gun. I'll take that window, Susan. You reload for us."

Buchanan said, "When you're ready that'll be fine. First some whiskey and a bit o' rest."

"I think I got one of them," said Peter Wolf. His eyes were round and wide. "I tried to get Wilder."

"Hard man to get," said Buchanan, "Just take it easy for a while."

He went back to watching. There were clouds forming overhead, and this worried him the most. Darkness would be an ally to the enemy. The room was full of shadows and the faint odor of fresh blood. One more gun wasn't enough to protect the perimeter of the house from a bold and sudden sortie with explosives.

Two safe, he thought, Johnnybear and Claire Robertson. For the rest he had fears. Wilder was the key. He only wished that Peter Wolf had been successful.

Wilder blew cigar smoke. Jake was still drinking. The woman came down from the buckboard and shrugged her shoulders.

"He keeps sayin' no dynamite. Account of the women. He's strong on not hurtin' the women."

"What does he think this is, a Sunday school picnic?"

"He'll be out of it soon," she said. "I know him. When he gets drinkin' like this he can't stop."

"I believe you. He's run his race, you know."

"Who knows better'n me?"

"If he was finished, it would just be the girl, Claire."

She laughed. "A handsome fella like you could handle her, now couldn't you?"

"You have ideas, don't you, Mrs. Bacon?"

"Just so you get Buchanan outa the way."

"That's the general idea. What do you think of the fat man?"

"The prospector? He hates Buchanan."

Wilder looked at the hulking stranger. He had come in with his dilapidated horse and a pack mule, babbling about a dog and Buchanan. He was leaning on a rifle, waiting.

She said, "He don't look like much."

"He is not much. He does have dynamite and caps that we need, though. No use getting in Buchanan's range, you know."

She said, "You want me to do anything?"

"You might talk to him. Nice and soft. You know how. He hasn't even seen a woman in a long while."

"You go on!" she said, pleased. "You think I could?"

"No doubt about it." Wilder watched her sidle up to the stranger. It was a laughable sight, but it might work. If she could work the man up to being reckless, it would be perfect.

Jake was bellowing, "Where's she at? Where's 'at woman with my bottle? Wilder, where you at?"

"Right here. Take another drink, Jake. It'll make you feel better."

"No dynamite. You unnerstand? Wait 'em out. When it's dark enough, we go in."

"Sure, Jake. Here's your bottle. Sure enough."

Wilder went back to his horse. If they could break down one wall, he thought, they would have a chance at Buchanan, who would do any reckless thing to protect the women. Once he was out of the way everything would be easy.

Wilder had no real ambition to take over the girl and the ranch. What he enjoyed was triumph. If he got Buchanan, he could travel the glory road. No matter how it was accomplished, he would take the credit. His head swam in dreams of glory.

It was twenty miles to the reservation. Johnnybear had to stop finally to get back his breath. He was in the forest now and safe from gunfire. It was the only place he could think of going, back to the Crow. Crazy Bird and the remaining young braves could help. The old people would be against it, he knew. It depended upon how they reacted to the hanging of Walking Elk.

Maybe they didn't mourn Walking Elk, because he had disobeyed the orders of the old men. Maybe Crazy Bird and the others were now under arrest. There were Crow scouts working for the army. The Crow had their own forces of order. He had to figure out which way to proceed. He did not believe the old ones would listen to talk from a boy, especially a boy dwelling among the whites.

The plight of the Caseys made him tremble despite himself. If nothing else, he promised the trees around him, he would go back and die with them or avenge them in some fashion.

The wind came from the mountains. The stars vanished one by one. The moon was obscured. Buchanan's heart sank. It was dark in the house, so no one could safely move about. He cautioned them and groped his way into the kitchen. The dogs made small sounds.

Mrs. Bower said, "You reckon the barn is first?"

"Uh-huh," said Buchanan.

Sandy, the one-eyed dog, woofed and rubbed against Buchanan's leg.

"There's someone out there," he said. "Behind the damn barn. I got a notion . . ."

He never finished. There was a puff, an explosion that rocked the earth. A blinding flash of light showed the barn going to pieces, one stone after the other. Buchanan said, "They played it smart. Now they got protection."

He leaned through a broken window and sprayed lead into the night. Mrs. Bower joined him. Sandy lurched at the door, barking. Buchanan played a hunch and opened it. The dog went straight past the barn. In a moment there was a yell and the fat stranger came into the light of burning hay and straw. The dog had his teeth fastened into his leg. The man screamed again and Buchanan shot him. He fell into the fire. The dog wheeled and came back to the house unharmed.

Buchanan said, "Never threaten a sheep dog, seems like."

"Who was that jasper?" Mrs. Bower asked.

"A miserable drifter. A prospector, I'd guess. Wilder knew how to use him."

"They'll have to wait for the fire to die down," she said.

"They can wait."

"They got to move before daylight."

"It's not yet midnight," he told her.

"If they do fort up in the barn, then what?"

"Then they'll try some more dynamite, prob'ly," said Buchanan. "If it stays dark as it is now, they got a chance."

"Not before we kill a few."

He said, "You're sure a cool one, lady. Bless you."

Buchanan made his way back into the parlor. He told them, "It ain't good, no matter how you look at it. Shoot anything that moves out there."

"The darkness," mourned Susan. "If I could just see them."

Casey said, "If they get to the house with dynamite . . ."

"If they do, we'll leave," Buchanan promised him. He did not say where they would go. His shoulder was hurting and his patience was growing short. It was all right to admonish the others, but he could not hold out much longer himself. He felt Coco beside him.

Coco whispered, "I'm goin' with you."

"Not yet."

"They gonna come in. This black night, they can't see us any better than we can see them."

"Don't let the others know," said Buchanan. Coco, as usual, was reading his mind.

Peter Wolf was at a window in the bedroom. Shawn Casey and his daughter each held another side of the house. Mrs. Casey was trying to maintain calm on the fourth side. It was a pitifully weak defense against Wilder and the men he commanded.

Buchanan hunkered down in the dark and waited. He rotated his left arm with care, trying to work out the pain. He silently slid out of his heavy cartridge belt and put his rifle aside. He filled his pockets with ammunition for his revolvers and loosened the bowie in its scabbard.

* * *

Claire Robertson talked to Dr. Abrams and his wife. Bascomb and others from the town listened without expression. The saloon was crowded, but the people were cowed.

When the explosion took place, the air shivered, the sky lit up. Claire's voice broke as she cried, "My God, they've gone mad! They've killed them all! Now will you come with me?"

The townspeople were startled. They stared around at one another. One or two shuffled their feet. A voice said. "It ain't right nohow." Bascomb picked up his shotgun but stood, irresolute, behind the bar.

Claire said, "My father wouldn't do that. It's that man Wilder and the woman. My father's woman. They're doing it."

"Your pa's drunk most o' the time," said a farmer.

"I know. But he wasn't always like that. If you'd all come and help . . . Oh, please. I'll ride ahead of you. He won't let them harm me. Please!"

They muttered to one another. They milled around talking, talking. They did not start for their horses or carriages or wagons. Dashing out of the saloon, Claire burst into tears.

She wept apart so that they would not know. Then she went back to them and redoubled her pleas.

Buchanan said, "If you folks don't hear me, just keep watch. I'll be moseyin' around."

"Where? What are you up to?" asked Susan.

"Don't fret. Just watch and shoot anything that comes at us."

He went into the kitchen. He found Mrs. Bower in the pitch-dark and put his lips close to her ear. "You got any shoe blackin'?"

She giggled. "Last time I looked you were wearin' brown boots."

"It ain't funny."

She asked, "Are you goin' out there?"

"Uh-huh." She leaned against him. She was very soft, yet her body was firm and strong. "It's plumb loco. And yet it ain't. They might could blow us apart."

"Blacking for my face and hands."

"I can do better. Wait just a few minutes." She moved across the room. She opened the oven door and lit a tiny candle. She was like a cat in the dark, he thought. He saw that she had a cork on a long fork.

Coco said, "I'm peelin' off my shirt. Let 'em try to see me in the dark."

It was best to see the funny side, Buchanan thought, but the job ahead was grim. If the wind changed and the moon and stars came out, the finish coud come in a few moments.

The tiny flame did not illuminate the room, but he could make out shapes. The lamb lay quiescent in a corner. The dogs stirred and again Sandy came to him. The dogs, he remembered, did not bark; they were trained not to alarm the herd of sheep. Two of them were fighters. Sandy was a veteran, wise to the ways of the plains.

Mrs. Bower came with the cork, immediately had another in the fire. He applied the blacking to his face. He wondered if it would be slippery on his hands—that he could not dare to risk. His mind worked methodically over what had to be done.

When she was ready with the second cork, he tried it on the back of his hands, decided against dyeing his palms. The candle was extinguished.

She said, "You could get clean away if you wanted."

"Uh-huh."

"So go with God." Her hand gripped his arm.

"We'll need His help and that of the devil," he told her.

They opened the door and slid out, Buchanan in the lead. Coco had learned through the years to follow him by day or night. They waited while the dogs filed out with them, then made straight away for the ruins of the barn. The dogs were close by but not too close, Buchanan thought. They were sniffing the odors of fire and burning, smoldering hay and straw.

Like all consummate plainsmen, Buchanan was a keen observer. Once over a piece of ground, he could remember every stone, every stalk of grass thereon. He knew precisely how many yards lay between house and barn. One revolver in hand, the other thrust into his Levi's, he worked his way to the ruins.

The earth was steaming from the conflagration. The air reeked with strong odors, worst of all that of the burning flesh of the fat prospector. Sandy growled low. Buchanan flattened himself to the ground.

Dave Dare's voice said, ''Get behind that big stone and light the lantern. Careful, now.''

''We light up and Buchanan shoots hell outa us, '' said someone.

''Got to have it. Think I can handle this stuff in the dark?''

''It won't go off without the caps. Tricky damn stuff.''

''I can manage. Put it down behind there. Got to get closer.''

''Too damn close.''

''Wilder sets there and gives orders. He ain't takin' any chances, now, is he?''

''Jake's drunk again. What the hell we gonna do, him and the damn woman drunk?''

''You heard Wilder. He'd as soon cut down on us if we don't do like he says.''

''Yeah, and if we do, look what happened to McGee and Semple.''

''We got orders. There just ain't any way out of it now.''

There were three of them, all Cross Bar riders, Buchanan realized. Wilder was saving his own killers for the finish.

Coco touched his arm. "You're best at sneakin' around. I go right in."

Buchanan estimated the odds. The dog at his side moved when he did, a good sign. He nodded agreement to Coco and with the dog crawled over broken stones through blackened straw. He felt a twinge in his shoulder. He saw the small light of the dark lantern and proceeded even slower. It was crucial that he make no sound to alert Wilder and his gunmen.

He felt the dogs nearby and put out a hand to steady them. He came close enough to see a box, which unquestionably held the dynamite. He tucked away his Colt. He took a deep breath. The timing must be exact or all was lost.

He went forward with a rush. He struck Dare behind the collar and whirled. Coco was throttling the second cowboy. Buchanan reached for the third.

The last man was covered by dogs. They had him down and were nuzzling at his throat. He tried to yell.

Buchanan hit him on the chin. He lost consciousness.

Coco asked, "Now we got 'em, what we do with 'em?"

"Stuff their mouths with their rebozos," said Buchanan. He went to where the dim silhouettes of hobbled horses wandered nearby and selected lariats. He came back and remembered knots an old salt had taught him one time in San Francisco. He trussed up the three semiconscious victims and stored them out of sight. It was then he noted that the wind was changing.

He said, "Now it's time to hustle. The less light on us the better. Take the lantern. Close the slide but keep it handy."

Coco said, "You reckon we can find all those jaspers in time?"

"I reckon we got to."

There was sporadic firing of guns. Flashes came from the roof where Gowdy and Indian Joe were holding out. The wind suddenly became a gale. A slice of moon peered down upon the scene. Two horsemen came toward the house riding like Comanches. They separated. The gunfire increased.

Buchanan said, "Grab a couple of sticks of that dynamite. Cap them and follow me."

He began to run. The horsemen were swifter. Shots from the house did not prevent them from coming close.

Each of the men on horseback reared back and threw objects. Buchanan said, "Too damn late."

He was not close enough to find a target for his short guns. He ran as fast as he could. Coco was still with the cache of explosives. One of the thrown objects fell near the house and sizzled. Choking, Buchanan ran toward it.

The door opened. Staggering, Peter Wolf appeared. The moon showed more light. Wilder's men concentrated their gunfire.

Peter Wolf reached the dynamite stick before Buchanan could get to it. He picked it up. The fuse burned close. Peter Wolf reached back and threw it far into the night. It exploded in midair. He turned to go back, stumbled and fell. Buchanan picked him up on the run. Lead tore through the air around them.

Susan was at the door. Buchanan came through. She slammed it behind him.

Peter Wolf was smiling in the moonlight. There was another hole in his chest. They put him on the couch and Susan leaned over him.

He said, "They . . . can't . . . get that . . . close. No good . . ."

She said, "Peter, don't talk. You'll be okay. Just don't try to talk.

Blood seeped from one corner of his mouth. He still smiled. He said, "You do . . . what . . . you got to do . . ."

Buchanan turned away, wiping tears from his eyes. His face hardened. He picked up his rifle and went wordlessly from the house. Coco was staying close to the wall, in a shadow.

Coco said, "They got him, didn't they?"

"They got him."

Coco looked at the capped dynamite sticks in his hands. "Tom, I don't shoot people. It ain't right. But the ladies. Peter Wolf. Walking Elk."

Buchanan said, "Look into your heart, pardner. Into your heart."

Buchanan walked toward the ruins of the barn, past the bound men on the ground. He whistled.

Nightshade came on a trot. The stars were showing their twinkling heads but he did not notice. He tightened the cinch and adjusted the bridle. A voice called to him, "Buchanan!"

It was Susan. She carried her rifle and wore her revolver around her waist.

He said, "Go back there!"

"Peter died," she said. "He was able to say one last thing. To me."

"Go back, girl!"

"He told me he loved me."

"You knew that."

"He died for me," she said.

"No reason for you to die."

"You heard him. 'You do what you got to do.' "

Buchanan said, "I heard him."

"You're doin' what you got to do."

"Damn it, girl . . ." But he could see it all, see into her head and heart. "I'm going to ride around them."

"I'm going to stay here and make sure they don't get into the barn like before."

He said, "The good Lord protect you, girl."

Words had become useless. He gave Nightshade his head and went westward. The fleet horse covered ground in great leaps. Out of view of the attackers, Buchanan reined in. He attached the leather reins to the horn of the saddle. He held the rifle in his right hand and a revolver in his left. He was now behind Robertson's group. Their numbers had been reduced, but the most dangerous fighters still were able.

He sat a moment in thought. In the house—and on the roof—were people who were not skillful marksmen. Coco was in shadows but vulnerable. The girl was outside where a stray bullet could kill her.

It was his style to charge. No matter the odds, no matter the wounds he had suffered, he had always been the aggressor. This time he dared not fail. Yet he knew the odds were against him. He pondered his strategy.

Johnnybear was standing straight, talking to the old ones on the reservation. "Buchanan has been a friend to the Crow. The Caseys have been good to me, to the half-Crow, Peter Wolf. The cattle people hanged Walking Elk. All I ask is your young men."

The oldest chief said, "What you say is true. But if we interfere, the soldiers will come. All will be blamed on us. The young men, they are doing penance. We cannot do as you ask."

Johnnybear stood taller. "Then give me a gun and a horse and let me die with my friends."

There was a silence. Then Crazy Bird walked into the circle. He said, "My blood brother died on a tree. It was a tree that once was in our forest, on Crow Land. Old men, you cannot stop us. We will go!"

The other young braves came with horses, one for Johnnybear. The old men puffed their pipes. They did not say more. The little band rode out.

In the town Claire was losing her voice. Now Bascomb and Dr. Abrams were also talking. The townsfolk still shifted from one foot to the other.

A woman cried, "For shame! If the cattlemen win, we'll be next. They've already showed us what they are."

Bascomb said, "If we ride out, they can't stop all of us."

"Some of us will be stopped," said a farmer. "I got a family."

"Sooner or later you won't have a farm," said Dr. Abrams. "Robertson wants every foot of land for his cattle."

"The man Wilder don't know mercy," said Bascomb. "I never was no brave man, but this time we got to do somethin'."

Claire said hoarsely, "My own father. I'm begging you against my own father."

They stirred. They began to move toward wagons, buckboards, saddle horses. The moon shone down upon them, a town in motion.

Time was skipping away for Buchanan. If he could see Wilder's men, then they could see him. Fortunately they were busy attending to their front, scattering as before. He knew they were carrying capped dynamite sticks. They were reckless men, and Wilder was a commanding leader. He could not hesitate much longer. He began to ride.

There was a movement near the buckboard where Jake sat with his bottle. Wilder raised his arm. A shower of sparks fluttered.

Horrified, Buchanan saw the explosion, saw the buckboard come apart, saw Jake hurtled into the air. He saw the woman safely away from the blast. He saw Wilder lift his arm again, a signal for his men to go into action.

Buchanan rode. He deliberately held his fire. He came riding in behind Wilder.

He called, "Here I am, Wilder!"

Wilder spun. The moonlight rode him. There was a cheroot in his mouth. His hand dipped for his holster.

Buchanan shot him in the arm.

Wilder tried for the second gun. Buchanan, now in close, whipped out with the barrel of his rifle. He caught Wilder alongside the head.

Buchanan was afoot before Wilder hit earth. With quick hands he disarmed the fallen figure. He looked close. Wilder was bleeding from the skull. Buchanan made a quick job of hog-tying him.

There was no time to look to Jake, to heed the screams of Mrs. Bacon. He leaped aboard Nightshade and rode.

The gunslingers were circling. They were getting close by jigsaw riding. Buchanan got within range. There was no pity in him. He aimed and fired. A rider slid from the saddle, his foot caught in the stirrup. He was dragged by the frightened horse, his head bumping along the ground.

The others were closing in. Gunfire came from the roof, the house. Still they circled, unaware of the loss of their leader. One came around the corner of the barn. Another came close to the house.

Buchanan could see Coco. He was leaning back, then forward, his powerful arm swinging. A stick of dynamite floated, seemed to hang on the air.

The rider near the house saw it coming, tried to swerve. A blinding flash caught him. Horse and rider went down in a tangle.

There was a shot from the rear of the house, then another. Buchanan rode for a running figure. The man saw him, threw the dynamite away, tried to bring his rifle into play.

Buchanan shot him through the chest, then swung around and headed for the barn. The rider who had made it there had turned loose Dave Dare and his companion. Susan was kneeling, firing at them. Once more a dangerous explosive soared high toward the roof of the house.

Buchanan lifted the rifle. He fired once, twice.

The dynamite exploded at the peak of its arc. Susan again pulled the trigger and a man screamed. Coco came around the corner of the house and once more let loose with his powerful arm. The dude called Reck stopped in mid-tracks and tried to run. The force of the blast sent him sprawling. Coco was on him, punching.

Buchanan scanned the field. The Bacon woman was wringing her hands over the prone figure of Wilder. For a moment Buchanan hoped she would cut him loose, that Wilder would arise for a last confrontation, armed and ready. Then he shrugged and wiped his face with his bandanna. He rode to the scene, looked again at the wreckage of the buckboard, at the inert Jake Robertson. The woman turned on him, screaming curses. He pointed to the house.

"Get over there, woman. You've done your worst."

"If Fritz was able . . . If Jake was alive . . ."

"Get goin'," he said wearily. She went with head bowed, weeping and wailing.

Wilder stared up at him. "You got a habit of ruining a man's arm, haven't you, Buchanan?"

"Sometimes."

"Nasty trick."

"It'll work, sometimes. Thing is, you'll get it in the neck, too."

"They don't hang you for killing Indian horse thieves," Wilder said.

"That's what you think."

"I didn't kill anyone else."

"Jake," said Buchanan.

"Prove it."

Buchanan said, "I saw you, Wilder."

The man scowled. Then he said, "Untie me and I'll draw on you left-handed."

"Too easy," said Buchanan. "I liked it better the other way."

He turned his back and rode to where Susan and Coco awaited him. Gowdy and Indian Joe had come down from the roof. They were bleeding from slight wounds but cheerful. The dogs gathered around them.

Susan said, "We'll get the doctor."

There was the sound of voices, people in wagons. They came from the direction of the town, brandishing weapons, shouting. They looked brave, even menacing in the moon-light.

"A little late," said Buchanan. "And look yonder."

Johnnybear was leading the four Indians. They rode in and stopped.

Buchanan said, "So that's where you went, boy."

"It took too much time."

Crazy Bird was staring at the wrecked buckboard, at Wilder on the ground. "Is he dead?"

"No."

"Can we take him?"

"No. The law will do it for you."

"White man's law."

"This time it will do the job."

"Prison?"

"Hangin'."

"For killing Walking Elk? Pah!" Crazy Bird spat.

"That's what he said. But he killed the cattleman, too."

"Yes. Killing a white man. He will hang."

"The way it is," said Buchanan.

"What honor does that give us?"

"You came here to help. That is honorable."

"We came for revenge."

Buchanan sighed. "No matter. Go now before the soldiers hear about it."

The Indians rode. It was better they had not been here earlier, Buchanan knew. Whatever their intent, there would be whites who would resent them. The trials and tribulations of the Indian were far from alleviated. He wondered if they ever would be.

Still wiping the blacking from his face, he rode to where the townspeople were milling about. Claire Robertson was with Susan Casey. Shawn and his wife were somewhat lost amid all the confusion. Buchanan dismounted and took Mrs. Bacon by the elbow. Claire faced them.

"Papa?"

"Wilder did it," whined the woman. "Wilder wanted to steal everything."

"Wilder wanted to kill everyone," Buchanan corrected her. "I'm terribly sorry, Claire."

"Where is my papa?"

Bascomb came by. Buchanan said to him, "Take care of Miz Bacon. I think she belongs in jail."

He went with Claire to where her father lay. She asked, "Peter?"

"Sorry."

"Dead?"

He nodded. She looked at her father's body. Broken whiskey bottles were strewn about him. She wheeled around to where Wilder lay.

Buchanan caught her hand before she could draw her revolver. "Not yet. Let the hangman do it for us."

She sagged against him. "I would have done it. I would have killed him."

"You'd be sorry. Better this way." Some men were coming with a wagon. "Let him ride to town with the others. They're all dead but him and Dave Dare and a couple who ran away."

"Armageddon." Her voice was very small.

"You'll live with it," he told her. "You can do it."

"Will I?"

"Things won't be the same. But you'll live," Buchanan told her.

"Can I make things right?"

"Nobody can do that. What you can do is try."

"The Caseys?"

"All alive. There, you see? You're thinkin' about other people already."

Dr. Abrams was busy with his little black bag. Bascomb had managed to take charge of the townsfolk, ordering them here and there in an attempt to restore some kind of order. A carpenter and a mason were already measuring the house for repairs. Shawn Casey was smiling and offering thanks in his gentle manner.

Susan came to Claire. Buchanan went with them into the house. Peter Wolf's body, covered by a clean sheet, lay upon the couch in the parlor. The piano was scarred by gunfire; the pictures on the wall were shattered. Coco came with the dark lantern still secure in his grasp. Mrs. Casey managed to light a lamp.

Claire lifted the sheet. For a long moment she looked at Peter Wolf. She did not shed a tear. When she turned away, Susan and Mrs. Casey were on either side of her. She smiled faintly at them and stepped back, standing alone.

"There will be no more trouble. You know that," she said. "That this should have happened . . . what can I say? We'll be friends. Believe me, we'll be friends." Her voice caught, then went on strongly again. "My father made a terrible mistake. He never had enough. He wanted more when more wasn't necessary. I . . . I think I'd better take him home now."

Buchanan said, "Coco . . . Johnnybear. See if you can manage a wagon, whatever is needed."

Claire drew herself up. "Would you mind . . . Father started this little graveyard . . . could I . . . Is there any reason Peter should not be buried there?"

"No reason," said Susan Casey. "No reason at all."

The Caseys surrounded the bereft girl. Buchanan slid into the kitchen. There was water in the sink. He saw himself in a cracked mirror.

"Look like the end man in a minstrel show," he muttered. He washed as best he could.

"Baaa."

He looked at the little black sheep in its corner. It was shivering with fear of the noise and confusion. "You," he said, "You're the cause of it all."

Beth Bower came in through the bullet-riddled door. "I heard that."

"It's true, ain't it?"

"Certainly it ain't," she scolded him. "Which you know 's well as I do."

"Uh-huh."

"People ain't so bad." She was at the stove again. "They're goin' to put up the barn for the Caseys. They feel bad about gettin' here late so they're goin' to repair everything in the house. Leastways they're promisin'."

"People do learn. They find there's things they got to do."

She came across the room. She looked up into his eyes. "You keep sayin' 'uh-huh.' You keep doin' the things that got to be done. But you don't like most of it."

"You're a right bright lady," he told her.

She put her arms around him and lifted her face. "You're a right fine man."

Over her shoulder he saw Susan in the doorway. She paused there for a moment and then was gone. He kissed Beth Bower.

TEN

BUCHANAN RODE A BORROWED HORSE UP INTO THE
Big Horns. Nightshade was back in New Mexico on the Button Ranch. The tracks were plain but it was not the bull elk,
he knew. He came down to the foothills and surveyed the
scene. He swung his arm. There was no pain. There was a
slight mark on his neck where Cobber had applied the steel
chain, but it gave him no trouble.

Down below a herd of Cross Bar cattle grazed. To the
north there were sheep. Barbed wire was not in evidence.
All the land was fair and the inevitably blue bowl of the Wyoming sky showed traces of wispy clouds lazily changing
patterns in high winds.

He had returned to testify against Fritz Wilder and Liz
Bacon. The one was to be hanged, the other jailed as an accessory before and after the murder of Jake Robertson. It
had not been a pleasant duty, but justice demanded it of him.
It had been good to see the town of Sheridan again a peaceful community, with Dr. Abrams as mayor and Bascomb on

the town council. In short months the community had grown, the farms had prospered, and all was serene.

He rode down to the sheep. Gowdy and Indian Joe greeted him. He shared a biscuit and Black coffee with them. The dog named Sandy came to nuzzle him.

He said, "And the black sheep has turned into a damn ram. Little Tommy Button can scarcely handle him anymore."

"God, it's the way of things," said Gowdy. "The country's gettin' full up. Everything changes."

"Exceptin' the Crow," said Indian Joe.

"Well, now, they're quiet," Gowdy put in. "We send 'em a few woolies now and then. Crazy Bird, he still hunts, but he don't steal nothin'."

"Uh-huh," said Buchanan. The coffee was black and rancid. "Peace. It's wonderful."

He said his good-byes and rode back to the Casey ranch. The barn was rebuilt; the house was intact except for a few bullet scars in the stone. Johnnybear came for the horse. He had grown two inches. Beth Bower was in the doorway to the kitchen, her hands folded in her apron. She was smiling.

Buchanan asked her, "Everything okay?" "It is now that you're here."

"But not for long." He was truly regretful.

She came close to him. 'Just once in a time, Buchanan. Just so you don't forget."

"Not likely." They went indoors. They kissed. "No way I could forget. You made the bad time go away."

Susan was playing the piano. They went into the parlor. There was cold food and whiskey and wine, and happy faces abounded. A carriage pulled up and Claire Robertson descended. She was dressed for town, but her white skin was now tanned and her stride had lengthened. She embraced Buchanan, then the Caseys one by one.

She said, "Dave Dare sends regards. He turned out well.

I'm glad to have him back. Cobber has a wooden leg. He did not send regards.''

Buchanan touched his neck. "And the same to him. It's real good to be with you-all."

Shawn Casey said, "There's a new preacher in town. Too bad you can't meet him. They're building a church."

"What does Buchanan care about such things?" Susan was blushing.

Mrs. Casey said, "They have one of those wheezy organs. Susan is learning to play it."

"That's enough," said Susan.

"The preacher hasn't proposed," Claire confided. "Susan is worried."

"I am not!" Susan sipped straight whiskey. "He either does or he don't. And anyway, there's a buyer that you haven't met. He asked me to supper."

"Looks like things are pickin' up all over," said Buchanan. He looked at Claire. "What about you?"

"I'm busy." There was an undertone of sadness. "Too busy to think about men. Papa left a lot of business that must be taken care of."

"You'll be fine." Buchanan went to her and put an arm around her. "You've got the good times comin'."

He picked up his carpetbag. He went around to them all, embracing them. They were gentle people in the best sense of the word.

Claire said, "Shall we go? You just have time to make the stage."

"Uh-huh." He took one last look before getting into the carriage. It was a lovely scene. Mrs. Bower blew him a kiss. Claire clucked at the team. They drew slowly away. He was returning to New Mexico, where Coco was training for a fight at Billy Button's spread. He would be happy there for the time allowed.

There would be only one thing missing. Beth Bower would be in Wyoming.